U0079388

就是
這一本 **超實用的**

旅遊 SO EASY 英語

國家圖書館出版品預行編目資料

就是這一本，超實用旅遊英語 / 雅典英研所編著
-- 初版. -- 新北市：雅典文化，民111.01
面；　公分. -- (全民學英文；63)
ISBN 978-626-95008-8-8(平裝)

1. 英語　2. 旅遊　3. 會話
805.188　　　　　　　　　　　　　110018924

全民學英文系列　63

就是這一本，超實用旅遊英語

編著／雅典英研所
責任編輯／張文娟
美術編輯／鄭孝儀
封面設計／林鈺恆

法律顧問：方圓法律事務所／涂成樞律師

總經銷：永續圖書有限公司
永續圖書線上購物網
www.foreverbooks.com.tw

出版日／2022年01月

a 雅典文化

出版社	22103　新北市汐止區大同路三段194號9樓之1 TEL　(02) 8647-3663 FAX　(02) 8647-3660

序言

　　本書是針對即將到英美語系國家旅遊的人所編寫，書中主要以會話的形式來介紹一些發生狀況時所必須用到的短句，由最基本的打招呼用語開始學習，不管是出國旅遊時問路、登機、逛街殺價、訂餐廳、向外國人介紹美麗的台灣、甚至遇到緊急狀況…有了這本「超實用的英語（旅遊）會話書」，您不用再害怕開口說英語，您可以搭配本書所附之外籍老師錄音，跟著開口覆誦練習，先習慣英文語感，在抵達英美語系國家時，希望您能多多利用本書，自由自在地開口說英語，留下更多與當地人互動的美麗回憶！

　　本書大綱分為十個大章節，每個章節再細分主題，主要以問與答的形式進行，除了教導讀者在什麼情境下使用此句型，也提供對話及相關例句。本書分類清楚，讓讀者能輕鬆找到需要使用的會話句型，並且以實用簡單為主，讓讀者能在出國時攜帶應用。

PART2
向外國人介紹台灣

PART3
機場與搭飛機

PART 4
交通與問路

PART 5
郵寄及電話用語

PART6
住宿

PART7
飲食

PART 8
購物

PART 9
觀光

PART 10
生病、意外狀況

Chapter

1

基本用語

track 01-01

Unit 1

打招呼

▶句型 A◀

- Hi!

  嗨!

- Hello!

  哈囉!

- Hey!

  嘿!

- What's up?

  近況如何?

會話實例

例 Hi! Sandy!

嗨!珊蒂!

例 Hey! John!

嘿!約翰!

▶句型 B◀

- Good morning!

  早安!

- Good afternoon!
  午安！

- Good evening!
  晚安！

- Good night!
  晚安！（睡前）

例 Good morning, teacher!
早安！老師！

例 Good morning, Sam!
早安！山姆！

track 01-02

Unit 2
問候

▶句型A◀

- How are you?
  你好嗎？

- How are you doing?
  你好嗎？

- How do you do?
  你好嗎？

- How have you been?
  你最近好嗎？

- How is everything?
  一切好嗎？

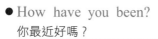

例 Hello!
  你好！

例 Hey! How are you doing?
  嘿！你近來好嗎？

例 Couldn't be better, and you?
  好極了。你呢？

例 Great.
  我很好。

▶ **句型 B** ◀

- I'm fine, thank you. And you?
  我很好，謝謝，你呢？

- Couldn't be better.
  好極了。

- Not bad.
  還不錯。

- So far so good.
  到目前為止都很好。

- Nothing special.
  老樣子。

- So so.
  馬馬虎虎。

- Not so good.
  不太好。

會話實例

例 How are you today?
你今天好嗎？

例 Not too bad.
還不錯！

track 01-03

好久不見

▶句型A◀

- Long time no see.
  好久不見！

- It's been ages since I last saw you!
  好久不見！

- I haven't seen you for a long time.
  好久不見！

會話實例

例 Alice?
　艾莉絲？

例 Hi! Jenny!
　嗨！珍妮！

例 Long time no see! Wow, you look great!
　好久不見！哇！你看起來好極了！

例 You, too! It's been so long! How have you been?
　你也是，好久不見，你最近好嗎？

例 I'm fine! And you?
　我很好，你呢？

例 Not bad.
　還不錯。

▶ 句型 B ◀

- It's great to see you!
  見到你真是太好了！

- I'm so glad to see you.
  見到你好開心。

- You look great!
  你看起來好極了！

會話實例

例 Elvin?
艾文？

例 Hi! Louis!
嗨！路易斯！

例 I haven't seen you for a long time.
好久不見！

例 It's great to see you!
見到你真是太好了！

track 01-04

Unit 4

介紹認識

►句型A◄

- What's your name?
  你叫什麼名字？

- May I have your name?
  請問大名？

- You are…?
  你是…?

- Your name, please?
  你是…?

- How do you spell your name?
  請問你的名字怎麼拼?

會話實例

例 I'm Yvonne. What's your name?
我是伊芳,你叫什麼名字?

例 Hi, Yvonne. My name is Linda.
嗨,伊芳,我叫琳達。

▶句型 B◀

- I am Mary.
  我是瑪莉。

- My name is Ann.
  我叫做安。

- Please call me Chuck.
  叫我查克就好。

- This is Dean.
  這是狄恩。

- Nice to meet you!
  很高興認識你!

會話實例

例 What's your name?

你叫什麼名字？

例 My name is Rebecca. Please call me Becky.

我叫做莉貝卡，叫我貝琪就好。

例 Hi, Becky. I'm Nathan. Nice to meet you!

嗨，貝琪。我叫納森，很高興認識你！

例 Nice to meet you, too.

我也很高興認識你。

🎧 track 01-05

Unit 5

道謝

►句型A◄

● Thank you!

謝謝你！

● Thank you so much!

非常感謝你！

- Thank you for calling.
  感謝你來電。

- Thank you for everything.
  謝謝你為我所做的一切。

- Thanks!
  謝拉!

- Thanks again!
  再次感謝你!

- I really appreciate it!
  我真的很感激!

會話實例

例 Thank you for the dinner.
   謝謝你招待的晚餐。

例 You are welcome.
   不客氣。

例 It's so nice of you. Thanks again.
   你人真是太好了,再次感謝你。

▶句型 B◀

- You are welcome.
  不客氣!(正式場合)

- My pleasure.
  這是我的榮幸。

- Don't mention it.
  不客氣！

- No problem!
  小意思！（非正式場合）

會話實例

例 Thank you for helping us.
謝謝你幫我們的忙。

例 Don't mention it.
不客氣！

Unit
6
問時間

 track 01-06

▶句型A◀

- What time is it?
  現在幾點？

- What time?
  什麼時候？

- When do you finish your work?
  你什麼時候下班？

會話實例

例 We're going to go shopping, would you like to come?

我們要去逛街，你要不要來？

例 I'd love to. What time?

好阿，幾點？

例 Two o'clock.

兩點。

例 Ok, see you then.

好的，到時候見。

▶句型 B◀

- It's six o'clock.

現在六點。

- It's late now.

時候不早了。

- Time is running out.

沒時間了！

- It's time to go.

該走了！

- Hurry up! We're late.

快點！我們遲到了！

● It's still early.
還很早。

會話實例

● What time is it now?
現在幾點？

● It's three thirty.
現在三點半。

● Hurry up! We're late.
快點！我們遲到了！

 ∩ track 01-07

Unit
7
道歉

▶句型A◀

● I'm sorry.
我很抱歉。

● I'm really sorry.
我真的很抱歉。

● I'm sorry to interrupt you.
很抱歉打斷你。

● I'm so sorry for this.
對這件事情我感到很抱歉。

1 基本用語

- I'm sorry for my rudeness.
  我為我的無禮感到抱歉。

- Please forgive me.
  請原諒我。

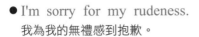

例 I'm really sorry for what I've done to you.
我為我對你所做的事深感抱歉。

例 Forget it.
算了。

▶句型B◀

- It's OK.
  沒關係。

- Never mind.
  沒關係。

- Forget it.
  算了。

- It's not your fault.
  這不是你的錯。

- Don't be sorry.
  你不必道歉。

- You don't have to apologize.
  你不必道歉。

會話實例

例 I'm really sorry to bother you.
很抱歉打擾你。

例 Don't be sorry. I'm glad to do it for you.
你不必道歉，我很樂意為你做這件事。

 🎧 track 01-08

Unit 8

道別

▶**句型A**◀

- Good-bye!
  再見！

- Bye-bye!
  再見！

- See you soon.
  再見！

- See you later.
  再見！

- See you next time.
  下次見！

- Catch you later!
  再見！

- I gotta go!
  我要走了！

會話實例

例 Bye!
再見！

例 See you later.
再見！

▶句型 B◀

- I hope to see you again.
  希望能再見到你。

- Nice talking to you!
  跟你聊天很開心！

- Good luck!
  祝你好運！

- Take care!
  保重！

- Have a nice day!
  祝你有美好的一天！

- Have a nice trip!
  祝你旅途愉快!

例 Let's keep in touch.

我們保持聯絡吧。

會話實例

例 I gotta go!

我要走了！

例 Take care!

保重！

🎧 track 01-09

Unit
9

沒聽清楚對方

▶句型 A◀

● Excuse me?

你說什麼？

● Pardon?

什麼？

● I beg your pardon?

請再說一次。

● What was that?

什麼？

● I didn't hear what you said.

我沒聽見你說什麼。

- I didn't catch what you said.
  我沒聽清楚你說什麼。

- What did you just say?
  你剛剛說什麼？

會話實例

例 I'm sorry. I didn't catch what you said.
我很抱歉，我沒聽清楚你說什麼。

例 I said, "please movc over."
我說「請移過去一點」。

▶句型 B◀

- I said, "Do you need my help?"
  我說「你需要幫忙嗎」？

- I said, "Would you mind to turn the volume down?"
  我說你介意開小聲一點嗎」？

- I said, "Please turn down the volume."
  我說「請關小聲一點」。

會話實例

例 Could you please turn the music down?
你可以把音樂開小聲一點嗎？

例 Excuse me?
你說什麼？

例 I said, "Could you please turn the music down?

例 I'm sorry, but I'm on the phone back here."
我說「你可以把音樂開小聲一點嗎？很抱歉，我正在後座講電話。」

例 I'm really sorry.
我很抱歉。

🎧 track 01-10

Unit 10
談論天氣

▶句型 A◀

● What's the weather like out there?
外面天氣怎樣？

● What's the weather going to be like?
天氣會如何？

● The weather is completely unpredictable.
天氣真是難以預測。

- Beautiful day, isn't it?
  天氣真好，對嗎？

- We had a downpour.
  我們剛遇到傾盆大雨。

會話實例

例 What's the weather going to be like to-morrow?
  明天天氣會如何？

例 Same as today.
  跟今天一樣。

▶**句型 B**◀

- It's really hot.
  真的很熱。

- It rained all day long.
  一整天都在下雨。

- It's raining heavily.
  雨很大。

- It's cold.
  很冷。

- It's chilly.
  超冷。

- It's freezing.
  冷斃了。

會話實例

例 What's the weather like out there?
外面天氣怎樣？

例 It's really hot.
真的很熱。

Unit
11
談論家人

▶句型A◀

- Who are they?
  他們是誰？

- Do you have any children?
  你有小孩嗎？

- Do you have any kids?
  你有小孩嗎？

- Do you have any brothers or sisters?
  你有兄弟姊妹嗎？

- How many siblings do you have?
  你有幾個兄弟姊妹？

- How many kids do you have?
  你有幾個小孩？

- How old is your son?
  你兒子幾歲？

- Do you live with your parents?
  你跟父母住在一起嗎？

會話實例

例 Do you have any children?
  你有小孩嗎？

例 I have a little girl and a little boy.
  我有一個小男孩和一個小女孩。

▶句型 B◀

- We're a family of four.
  我們家有四個人。

- I'm the youngest in my family.
  我是家裡最小的。

- I'm the only child in my family.
  我是獨生子。

會話實例

例 How many people are there in your family?

你們家有幾個人？

例 We're a family of four.

我們家有四個人。

例 Do you live with your parents?

你跟父母住在一起嗎？

例 Yes, I do.

是的。

track 01-12

Unit 12

談論興趣

▶句型A◀

● What do you usually do in your leisure time?

你閒暇時通常都在做什麼？

● Do you have any hobbics?

你有任何興趣嗎？

- Do you like football?
  你喜歡足球嗎？

- Do you watch basketball on TV?
  你會在電視上看籃球比賽嗎？

- Do you like jazz?
  你喜歡爵士樂嗎？

會話實例

例 What do you usually do in your leisure time?
你閒暇時通常都在做什麼？

例 I like to read novels and watch movies.
我喜歡看小說跟電影。

▶句型 B◀

- I love movies.
  我喜歡電影。

- My favorite sport is swimming.
  我最喜歡的運動是游泳。

- My favorite music is hiphop music.
  我最喜歡的音樂是嘻哈音樂。

- I like to go mountain climbing on weekends.
  我喜歡在週末去爬山。

- I go jogging every morning.
  我每天早上都去晨跑。

- I'm not interested in listening to jazz.
  我對爵士樂沒興趣。

- I like to go shopping.
  我喜歡去逛街。

- I like to spend my time with friends.
  我喜歡花時間和我的朋友在一起。

會話實例

例 Do you have any hobbies?
  你有任何興趣嗎？

例 I like to go mountain climbing on
  weekends.
  我喜歡在週末去爬山。

 track 01-13

Unit 13 談論工作

▶句型A◀

- What do you do?
  你從事什麼工作？

- What do you do, if I may ask?
  如果不介意我問，你從事什麼工作？

- What's your job?
  你從事什麼工作？

- What's business are you in?
  你從事哪一行？

- What's your position?
  你的職位是什麼？

- Where do you work?
  你在哪工作？

會話實例

例 What do you do?
  你從事什麼工作？

例 I am an engineer.
  我是工程師。

▶ 句型 B ◀

- How about you?
  你呢？

- I am a teacher.
  我是老師。

- I am an engineer.
  我是工程師。

- I am an editor.
  我是編輯。

- I am a designer.
  我是設計師。

- I work for a computer company.
  我在一家電腦公司上班。

- I've been jobless for more than 3 months.
  我已經失業三個多月了。

會話實例

例 What business are you in?
你從事哪一行？

例 I work for a computer company.
我在一家電腦公司上班。

 track 01-14

Unit 14

關心、安慰

▶句型A◀

- Are you OK?
  你還好吧？

- How do you feel now?
  你現在覺得如何？

- Is something bothering you?
  有什麼事困擾你嗎？

- I really worry about you.
  我真的很擔心你。

- Is there anything wrong?
  有問題嗎？

- Everything will be alright.
  一切都會順利的。

- You'll get through it.
  你會度過難關的。

- Take a deep breath.
  深呼吸一口氣。

會話實例

例 Are you OK?
  你還好吧？

例 I'm OK.
  我很好。

▶句型 B◀

- So so.
  還好。

- I'm OK.
  我很好。

- I think I failed it.
  我想我搞砸了。

- Just leave me alone.
  讓我一個人靜一靜。

會話實例

例 Is there anything wrong?
  有問題嗎?

例 I think I failed it.
  我想我搞砸了。

例 Do you want to talk about it?
  你想要談談嗎?

例 Please Just leave me alone.
  請讓我一個人靜一靜。

🎧track 01-15

Unit
15
關心病人

▶句型A◀

- Did you see a doctor?
  你有去看醫生嗎?

- How are you fccling now?
  你現在覺得如何？

- Are you feeling OK?
  你覺得好點嗎？

- How is your leg?
  你的腿還好吧？

- You look terrible.
  你的臉色看起來很糟。

- You look pale.
  你看起來很蒼白。

- You'd better get some rest.
  你最好多休息。

- You'd better lie down.
  你最好躺下來。

會話實例

例 Are you feeling OK?
你覺得好點嗎？

例 I feel better, thank you.
我好多了，謝謝。

▶句型B◀

- I sprained my ankle yesterday.
  我昨天扭到腳踝。

- My mom took me to the hospital.
  我媽有帶我去看醫生。

- I feel better.
  我好多了。

- Thanks for your concern.
  謝謝你的關心。

會話實例

例 You look pale. Did you see a doctor?
看起來很蒼白,你有去看醫生嗎?

例 My mom took me to the hospital.
我媽有帶我去看醫生。

例 Try to get some sleep.
試著睡覺吧!

 track 01-16

理解

▶句型A◀

- Are you following me?
  你懂我意思嗎?

- Don't you get it?
  你不懂嗎?

- Can't you see?
  你不瞭解嗎？

- Do you understand?
  你瞭不瞭解？

- Do you get it?
  你懂嗎？

- Is that clear?
  清楚嗎？

會話實例

例 Do you understand?
你瞭不瞭解？

例 Yes, I understand.
我瞭解。

▶句型 B◀

- I see.
  我懂了。

- I understand.
  我理解。

- I completely understand.
  我完全理解。

- I know what you're saying.
  我知道你在說什麼。

● I got you.
我懂你的意思。

會話實例

例 Do you get it?
你懂嗎？

例 I got you.
我懂你的意思。

🎧 track 01-17

Unit
17
邀請

▶ 句型 A ◀

● Do you want to come along?
你要一起來嗎？

● Come with us.
跟我們一起來吧！

● Let's go.
走吧！

● Wanna come along with us?
要跟我們一起去嗎？

- Would you like to join us?
  你要加入我們嗎?

- How about having dinner with me?
  跟我吃晚餐如何?

- Do you wanna go out for dinner tonight?
  今天晚餐要一起去外面吃嗎?

會話實例

例 Do you want to come along?
你要一起來嗎?

例 Sure, what time?
好啊,幾點?

▶句型B◀

- That sounds good.
  聽起來不錯!

- Good idea.
  好主意!

- That would be fine.
  應該不錯!

- I'd like to, but I have other plans.
  我很想,可是我有事。

- I'd love to, but I'm afraid I can't.
  我很想去,可是我恐怕不行。

- I'll let you know.
  我再跟你說。

- Maybe some other time.
  改天吧！

- I'm invited to Tom's party.
  我被邀請去湯姆的派對。

會話實例

例 I'm invited to tom's party.
我被邀請去湯姆的派對。

例 Have fun!
好好玩！

🎧 track 01-18

Unit 18

感到高興

▶句型A◀

- Congratulations!
  恭喜！

- I'm glad for you.
  我為你感到高興。

- Good for you.
  這對你很好。

- I'm glad you say so.
  我很高興你這麼說。

- I'm really happy for you.
  我真的為你感到高興。

- That's good news.
  真是好消息！

- That's too good to be true.
  好到令人不敢相信是真的！

- You're so lucky.
  你太幸運了！

會話實例

例 I just got a promotion!
  我升職了！

例 Congratulations!
  恭喜！

▶句型 B◀

- Let's celebrate.
  我們去慶祝！

- Maybe we should celebrate it.
  或許我們該慶祝一下！

- Let's go for a drink.
  我們去喝一杯！

會話實例

例 I just got a promotion!
我升職了！

例 I'm really happy for you.
我真的為你感到高興。

例 Let's go for a drink.
我們去喝一杯！

例 Sure.
好啊！

🎧 track 01-19

Unit 19

結束話題

▶句型A◀

- I've got to leave.
  我得走了。

- I've got to get back to work.
  我要回去工作了。

- I really need to be going.
  我真的要走了。

- It was nice talking to you.
  能和你談話真好。

- Talk to you later.
  下次再和你聊。

會話實例

例 I've got to get back to work.
  我要回去工作了。

例 See you soon.
  再見囉！

▶句型 B◀

- See you soon.
  再見囉！

- Take care.
  保重！

- Have a nice weekend.
  週末愉快！

- I'll let you go now.
  先這樣囉！

會話實例

例 I really need to be going.
  我真的要走了。

例 OK, talk to you later.

下次再和你聊。

Unit 20 讚美

▶**句型A**◀

- Good job!

  幹得好！

- Well done.

  幹得好！

- I'm proud of you.

  我以你為榮！

- Good boy!

  好小子！

- You are doing well.

  你做得很好！

- Excellent!

  真不錯！

- Awesome!

  真棒！

● Not bad!

不錯嘛！

會話實例

例 I just finished the annual plans.

我剛剛完成了年度企畫書。

例 Good job!

幹得好！

▶句型 B◀

● Thank you.

謝謝！

● Thank you for your encouragement.

謝謝你的鼓勵！

會話實例

例 Nice dress!

不錯的衣服喔！

例 Thanks.

謝謝！

 ⚏track 01-21

加油打氣

▶句型A◀

- Oh, come on.
  噢，別這樣嘛！

- Cheer up!
  高興點！

- You will make it!
  你可以辦到的！

- You can do it!
  你可以辦得到的！

- Take it easy!
  放輕鬆！

- Don't let me down.
  不要讓我失望！

- Do your best!
  你要盡力！

- I'm with you.
  我和你是同一陣線的。

會話實例

例 Do your best!
你要盡力！

例 OK.
好。

▶ 句型 B ◀

● Don't try to comfort me.
不要試圖安慰我。

● I'll do my best.
我會盡力的。

會話實例

例 Oh, come on.
噢，別這樣嘛！

例 Don't try to comfort me.
不要試圖安慰我。

● You can't go on like this.
你不能老是這樣下去。

你一定要聽懂的10句話

1. How are you?
   你好嗎？

2. Long time no see.
   好久不見！

3. What's your name?
   你叫什麼名字？

4. You are welcome.
   不客氣！

5. Never mind.
   沒關係。

6. Take care!
   保重！

7. Have a nice day!
   祝你有美好的一天！

8. Do you understand?
   你瞭不瞭解？

9. Do you want to come along?
   你要一起來嗎？

10. I've got to leave.
    我得走了。

你一定要會說的 10 句話

1. I'm fine, thank you. And you?
   我很好，謝謝，你呢？
2. My name is Ann.
   我叫做安。
3. Nice to meet you!
   很高興認識你！
4. Thank you so much!
   非常感謝你！
5. I'm sorry.
   我很抱歉。
6. Good-bye!
   再見！
7. Excuse me?
   你説什麼？
8. Are you OK?
   你還好吧？
9. I understand.
   我理解。
10. Talk to you later.
    下次再和你聊。

Chapter

2

向外國人介紹台灣

Unit 1 台灣在哪裡？

►句型A◄

- Where are you from?
  你從哪裡來？

- Where is Taiwan?
  台灣在哪裡？

- What is the population of Taiwan?
  台灣有多少人口？

- What's the weather like in Taiwan?
  台灣的天氣如何？

- What languages are spoken in Taiwan?
  台灣人說什麼語言呢？

會話實例

例 Where are you from?
你從哪裡來？

例 I'm from Taiwan.
我從台灣來。

例 Oh…I know… Thailand, right?
喔…我知道…是泰國嗎？

例 No, Taiwan and Thailand are different countries.

不是，台灣和泰國是兩個不同的國家。

► 句型 B ◄

● Taiwan is an island located off the southeastern coast of China.

台灣是一座位於中國東南沿岸的小島。

● The population of Taiwan is about 23 million.

台灣大約有兩千三百萬的人口。

● It's hot and humid in summer and cold in winter in Taiwan.

台灣夏天濕熱，冬天寒冷。

● We speak Mandarin Chinese, Taiwanese, Hakka and Formosan languages in Taiwan.

在台灣我們說中文、台語、客家話以及原住民語。

● Taiwan is used to be called Formosa. It means beautiful island.

台灣曾經被稱為福爾摩斯，意思是美麗之島。

- Taiwan is a melting pot of diverse ethnic cultures.

臺灣是多元族群與文化的大熔爐。

會話實例

例 Where is Taiwan?

台灣在哪裡？

例 Taiwan is an island located off the southeastern coast of China.

台灣是一座位於中國東南沿岸的小島。

 🎧 track 02-02

Unit 2 台灣美食

▶句型A◀

- Do you have any suggestions?

你有何建議嗎？

- What are the specialties of Taiwan?

台灣有什麼特別的美食嗎？

- Is there a good restaurant nearby?

附近有什麼好餐廳嗎？

會話實例

例 Do you have any suggestions?
你有何建議嗎?

例 You can't miss the specialties of Shilin night market.
你絕對不能錯過士林夜市的美食。

▶句型B◀

- What do you want to eat?
  你想要吃什麼?

- Let's go to Shilin night market.
  我們去士林夜市。

- Do you want to try our famous steamed dumplings?
  你要試試看我們有名的小籠包嗎?

- Have you ever tried stinky tofu?
  你有吃過臭豆腐嗎?

- Pearl milk tea is one of Taiwan's best-known specialty drinks.
  珍珠奶茶是最有名的台灣飲料之一。

- You must try small sausage in big sausage.
  你一定要嚐嚐看大腸包小腸。

- Hakka stir-fried meat is a home style delicacy you can't miss.
客家小炒是你不能錯過的美味家常菜餚。

會話實例

例 What are the specialties of Taiwan?
台灣有什麼特別的美食嗎？

例 Pearl milk tea is the beverage Taiwan is most known for.
珍珠奶茶是台灣最具代表性的飲料。

🎧track 02-03

Unit 3
台灣節慶

▶句型A◀

- Can you introduce me to some traditional festivals in Taiwan?
你能介紹我認識一些台灣的傳統節慶嗎？

- Why do Taiwanese people eat Tang Yuan on Lantern Festival?
台灣人為什麼要在元宵節吃湯圓呢？

會話實例

例 Can you introduce me to some traditional festivals in Taiwan?

你能介紹我認識一些台灣的傳統節慶嗎？

例 Sure. The upcoming festival is Mid-Autumn Festival. On this night people stay together for moon appreciation parties.

好的，即將來臨的節慶是中秋節，在這天晚上人們會聚在一起賞月。

例 That sounds great!

聽起來很棒！

▶句型 B◀

- Children who have left their hometowns return on New Year's Eve.

離開家鄉的孩子在除夕夜這天返家。

- Dragon Boat Festival is an occasion for driving off evil spirits and pestilences.

端午節是一個旨在驅邪避惡的節慶。

- Lantern Festival is celebrated by eating Tang Yuan, an important custom symbolizing family unity.

  大家吃湯圓來慶祝元宵節，這是一個象徵家庭團圓的習俗。

會話實例

例 Children who have left their hometowns return on New Year's Eve to share New Year's Eve Dinner with their families.

離開家鄉的孩子在除夕夜這天返家與人共享團圓飯。

例 It seems that reunion is very important to Chinese people.

看來團圓對中國人來說很重要。

🎧 track 02-04

Unit 4

台灣旅遊

▶ **句型A** ◀

- I'd like to go hiking. Could you give me some advice?

  我想去爬山健行，你能給我一些建議嗎？

- I want to take a trip around the island.

  我想要去環島旅行。

- I'd like to go to the National Palace Museum.

  我想要去參觀故宮博物館。

會話實例

例 I'd like to go hiking. Could you give me some advice?

我想去爬山健行，你能給我一些建議嗎？

例 You can go to Alishan, The Alishan National Scenic Area is a beautifully preserved mountainous area in central Taiwan.

你可以去阿里山，阿里山國家景觀區是一個在台灣中部的美麗山林保留區。

例 OK.

好啊。

例 The most picturesque way to reach the summit of Alishan is by the Alishan Railway.

通往阿里山山頂最美麗的一條路是阿里山鐵道。

向外國人介紹台灣

▶句型 B◀

- There are seven national parks in Taiwan.

  台灣有七座國家公園。

- The hot springs of the Yangmingshan and Beitou districts of Taipei is very famous.

  台北的陽明山和北投的溫泉很有名。

- You can enjoy snorkeling in the Pacific and rafting along the rapids of the Xiuguluan River.

  你可以在太平洋享受浮潛並且去秀姑巒溪玩急流泛舟。

- Tainan is famous for their historic monuments and local specialties.

  台南以他們的古蹟及地方小吃聞名。

- Kenting National Park features living coral reefs and diverse marine life.

  墾丁國家公園的特色是擁有珊瑚礁以及多樣化的海洋生態。

會話實例

例 How many national parks are there in Taiwan?

台灣有幾座國家公園？

例 There are seven national parks in Taiwan.

台灣有七座國家公園。

 track 02-05

你一定要聽懂的10句話

1. Where are you from?
   你從哪裡來？
2. Where is Taiwan?
   台灣在哪裡？
3. What is the population of Taiwan?
   台灣有多少人口？
4. What's the weather like in Taiwan?
   台灣的天氣如何？
5. What languages are spoken in Taiwan?
   台灣人說什麼語言呢？
6. What are the specialties of Taiwan?
   台灣有什麼特別的美食嗎？

7. Is there a good rcstaurant nearby?
   附近有什麼好餐廳嗎？

8. Can you introduce me to some traditional festivals in Taiwan?
   你能介紹我認識一些台灣的傳統節慶嗎？

9. I want to take a trip around the island.
   我想要去環島旅行。

10. I'd like to go to the National Palace Museum.
    我想要去參觀故宮博物館。

你一定要會說的 10 句話

1. I'm from Taiwan.
   我從台灣來。

2. I am Taiwanese.
   我是台灣人。

3. Taiwan is an island located off the sou theastern coast of China.
   台灣是一座位於中國東南沿岸的小島。

4. The population of Taiwan is about 23 million.
   台灣大約有兩千三百萬的人口。

5. What do you want to eat?
   你想要吃什麼？

6. Pearl milk tea is one of Taiwan's best-known specialty drinks.
   珍珠奶茶是最有名的台灣飲料之一。

7. We speak Mandarin Chinese, Taiwanese, Hakka and Formosan in Taiwan.
   在台灣我們說中文、台語、客家話及原住民語。

8. It's hot and humid in summer and cold in winter in Taiwan.
   台灣夏天濕熱，冬天寒冷。

9. There are seven national parks in Taiwan.
   台灣有七座國家公園。

10. Tainan is famous for their historic monuments and local specialties.
    台南以他們的古蹟及地方小吃聞名。

Chapter

機場與搭飛機

訂購機票

Unit 1 預約機位

▶句型 **A**◀

- Good morning. How can I help you?

  早安,我能為你做什麼?

- This is American Airlines. May I help you?

  這裡是美國航空,有什麼需要我效勞的嗎?

- What can I do for you?

  我能為你做什麼呢?

- Where do you plan to go?

  你計畫要去哪裡?

- When do you want to depart?

  您什麼時候出發?

- What time do you prefer?

  您偏好什麼時間?

會話實例

例 Good morning. How can I help you?
早安,我能為你做什麼?

例 I'd like to make a flight reservation.
我要預約機位。

例 Where do you plan to go?
你要去哪裡?

例 From Taipei to Paris.
從台北到巴黎。

▶句型 B◀

- I'd like to make a flight reservation.
  我要預約機位。

- I'd like to book a nonstop flight to London.
  我想要預訂到倫敦的直飛航班。

- I'd like a stopover flight.
  我要訂轉機的班機。

- I'd like to book the flight from Taipei to New York on May 5th.
  我想要預訂五月五號從台北到倫敦的班機。

- I'd like to book the first flight to Lyon for December 15th.
  我想要預訂十二月十五日到里昂的最早航班。

- I want to make a reservation from New York to Chicago.

  我要預約紐約到芝加哥的機票。

例 May I help you?

有什麼需要我效勞的嗎？

例 I'd like to book a flight from Taipei to London on September 3rd.

我想要預訂從九月三號從台北直飛倫敦的航班。

🎧track 03-02

Unit
2

詢問班機、價錢

▶句型A◀

- Do you fly to Tokyo on March 23rd?

  請問你們有三月23號到東京的班機嗎？

- Do you fly from Taipei to Tokyo on next Saturday?

  請問你們有下禮拜六從台北到東京的班機嗎？

- Could you check the boarding time for me?

  你能幫我查班機時刻表嗎？

- What's the next earliest flight for Hanoi?

  下一班最早到河內的班機是哪一班？

- How much is the airfare to Mexico?

  請問到墨西哥的機票多少錢？

- I'd like to know the airfare.

  我想知道票價。

- What's the fare from Bali to Singapore?

  請問從巴里島到新加坡的票價是多少錢？

會話實例

例 Do you fly to Madrid on May 20th?

請問你們有五月二十號到馬德里的班機嗎？

例 Let me check. Wait a moment, please.

我幫您查一下，請稍等。

▶句型 B◀

- Let me check. Wait a moment, please.

  我幫您查一下，請稍等。

- No problem, sir, please wait a moment.

  沒問題，先生，請稍等一下。

- We have a flight on March 23rd.
  我們三月23號有班機。

- Sorry, sir, we don't have any flights to Tokyo on Monday.
  很抱歉,先生,我們禮拜一沒有飛往東京的班機。

- I'm sorry, sir, that's the only flight we have.
  很抱歉,先生,那是我們僅有的一個班次。

- It's one thousand USD.
  一千美金。

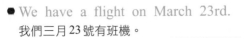

例 How much is the airfare to Vancouver?
請問到溫哥華的機票多少錢?

例 It's one thousand USD.
一千美金。

Unit 3 訂機票

▶句型 A◀

- I'd like to book a round-trip ticket.
  我要訂一張來回機票。

- Please leave the return ticket open.
  回程機票請不要限定班次時間。

- I'd like to book two seats.
  我要訂兩張機票。

- I'd like to book two seats from San Diego to New York.
  我要訂兩張從聖地牙哥到紐約的機票。

會話實例

例 I'd like to book a round-trip ticket.
我要訂一張來回機票。

例 Where do you plan to go?
你要去哪裡？

例 From Paris to Milan.
從巴黎到米蘭。

例 When do you want to depart?

您什麼時候出發？

例 I'm thinking of flying from Paris to Milan on December 23rd.

我打算十二月二十三號從巴黎出發到米蘭。

▶ 句型 B ◀

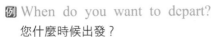

● Where do you plan to go?

你計畫要去哪裡？

● When do you want to depart?

您什麼時候出發？

● May I have your name, please?

請問你的大名？

● Please give me both of your names.

請給我兩位的名字。

會話實例

例 I'd like to book a round-trip ticket from Taipei to Sydney.

我要訂一張從台北到雪梨的來回機票。

例 May I have your name, please?

請問你的大名？

例 Cindy Foster.

辛蒂佛斯特。

∩ track 03-04

艙等、靠窗、走道

►句型 A◄

● Economy, Business class or First?
你要經濟艙、商務艙或頭等艙？

● Aisle or window seat?
走道還是靠窗？

● Where would you like to sit?
你想要坐哪裡？

● Do you have any seating preference?
你有特別想坐哪裡嗎？

● Would you like a window or an aisle seat?
你想要坐靠窗還是靠走道？

● There are no window seats left.
沒有靠窗的座位了。

會話實例

例 Would you like a window or an aisle seat?

你想要坐靠窗還是靠走道？

例 Please give me an aisle seat.

請給我靠走道的位置。

▶句型B◀

- I'd prefer an aislc seat.

  我偏好靠走道的坐位。

- I want a window seat.

  請給我靠窗的座位。

- I'd like an emergency exit seat.

  我想要靠近緊急出口的坐位。

- I'd like an aisle seat, but not a middle one, please.

  請給我靠走道的座位，但不要在中間。

- May I have a window seat?

  可以給我靠窗的座位嗎？

- Is it an aisle seat?

  是靠走道的位置嗎？

會話實例

- May I have a window seat?
  可以給我靠窗的座位嗎？

- Sure, no problem.
  好的，沒問題。

- That would be fine.
  太好了。

Unit 5
取消訂位

▶ 句型 A ◀

- I'd like to cancel my reservation
  我想取消我的訂位。

- I'd like to cancel a flight for Mr. Johnson.
  我想幫強生先生取消他的訂位。

- I'd like to change my flight.
  我想更改我的班機。

會話實例

例 I'd like to cancel my reservation

我想取消我的訂位。

例 OK, sir, please give me your name.

請給我您的名字。

▶句型 B◀

● Which date do you prefer to change?

您想要改成哪天呢？

會話實例

例 This is Cathay airlines. May I help you?

這裡是國泰航空，您需要什麼服務呢？

例 I'd like to change my flight.

我想更改我的班機。

例 Please give me your names.

請給我您的名字。

例 My name is Lin ling.

我的名字是林玲。

例 Which date do you prefer to change?

您想要改成哪天呢？

例 September 10th.

九月十號。

登機手續

登機報到

▶句型 A◀

- Where may I check in for my flight?
  請問哪裡可以辦理登機手續？

- Can I check in now?
  請問現在可以辦理登機手續嗎？

- Can I check in for flight VN 534 now?
  我可以辦理 VN 534 班機的登機手續嗎？

- Check-in, please.
  我要辦理登機。

- I'd like to check in.
  我要辦理登機。

會話實例

例 Where may I check in for my flight?
  請問哪裡可以辦理登機手續？

例 Let's me see your ticket.

我看看你的票。

例 Here you are.

這裡。

例 Go straight and turn right at the corner,
then you'll see it.

直走到轉角右轉，你就會看到了。

例 Thank you very much.

非常感謝你。

▶句型 B◀

● Lct's me see your ticket.

讓我看看你的票。

● May I have your passport and flight
ticket, please?

請給我您的護照跟機票。

● OK, sir. Passport and visa, please.

好的，先生。請給我護照跟簽證。

● Here's your boarding pass. Your seat is
52H.

這是您的登機證，您的座位是52H。

● Please be at gate 18 one hour before
the flight departs.

請在飛機起飛前一小時到達十八號登機門。

會話實例

例 Can I check in now?

請問現在可以辦理登機手續嗎？

例 Yes, may I have your passport and visa?

請給我你的護照跟簽證。

例 Here you are.

這裡。

track 03-07

登機手續

Unit 7

行李托運、超重

► 句型 A ◄

● I have two pieces of baggage to check in.

我有兩件行李要托運。

● How much is the extra charge?

請問超重費是多少？

● Is my luggage overweight?

我的行李有超重嗎？

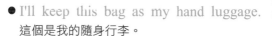

- I'll keep this bag as my hand luggage.
  這個是我的隨身行李。

- I just have this carry-on bag.
  我只有這件隨身背包。

會話實例

例 I have two pieces of baggage to check in.
  我有兩件行李要托運。

例 Please put your luggage on the scale.
  請把行李放在秤上。

▶句型B◀

- How many pieces of baggage do you have?
  你有幾件行李要托運？

- Do you have any baggage to check in?
  你有任何行李要托運嗎？

- You'll have to check in your bag.
  你的袋子需要辦理托運。

- It's too big to carry on.
  它太大了，不能帶上機。

- Please put your luggage on the scale.
  請把行李放在秤上。

3 機場與搭飛機

087

會話實例

例 Do you have any baggage to check in?
你有任何行李要托運嗎？

例 No. I'll keep this bag as my hand baggage.
這個是我的隨身行李。

🎧 track 03-08

Unit 8

登機時間

▶ 句型 **A** ◀

- What's the boarding time?
  登機時間是什麼時候？

- What time can we start boarding?
  我們什麼時候可以開始登機？

- What time will boarding start?
  什麼時候開始登機？

會話實例

例 May I help you?
需要我幫忙嗎？

例 What time can we start boarding?

我們什麼時候可以開始登機？

例 Let me see your boarding pass.

讓我看看你的登機證。

例 Here you are.

這裡。

例 At 9 o'clock, one hour before departure.

九點，起飛前一小時前。

▶ 句型 B ◀

● Let me see your boarding pass.
讓我看看你的登機證。

● You need to be at the gate by 10 am.
你需要在早上十點鐘前抵達登機門。

會話實例

例 What time will boarding start?
什麼時候開始登機？

例 Let me see your boarding pass.
讓我看看你的登機證。

例 You need to be at the gate by 10 am.
你需要在早上十點鐘前抵達登機門。

例 Thank you very much.
非常感謝你。

🎧 track 03-09

出境/登機

Unit 9

詢問登機門

▶ 句型 **A** ◀

● How should I get to terminal one?
請問第一航廈怎麼去？

● Where should I board?
我應該到哪裡登機？

● Where is the boarding gate?
登機門在哪裡？

● Which way is gate 17?
請問十七號登機門是在哪個方向？

● Can you direct me to gate 3, please?
可以請你告訴我怎麼去三號登機門嗎？

● I don't know where I should board.
我不知道我應該在哪裡登機。

● I'm at the wrong gate.
我走錯登機門了。

會話實例

例 Excuse me. How should I get to terminal two?

不好意思，請問第二航廈怎麼去？

例 Go straight ahead and you'll see it on your right side.

往前直走，你就會看到在你的右手邊。

▶句型 B◀

● Go straight ahead until the coffee shop and turn right, you'll find it.

直走到咖啡店右轉，你就會看到了。

● Take the escalator to level 2. Then turn right.

搭手扶梯到二樓，然後右轉。

● What's your gate number?

你的登機門是幾號？

● Let me see your boarding pass.

讓我看你的登機證。

會話實例

例 I don't know where I should board.

我不知我應該在哪裡登機。

例 Let me see your boarding pass.

讓我看你的登機證。

🎧 track 03-10

Unit 10

班機延誤

►句型A◄

● Can you tell me about my flight status?

你可以告訴我的班機情況嗎？

● Will the flight depart on time?

班機會準時起飛嗎？

● Is the plane on schedule?

飛機會準時嗎？

● Is the flight delayed?

飛機會誤點嗎？

● When is the new boarding time?

新的登機時間是幾點？

● Where is the new boarding gate?

新的登機門在哪？

● Do you give lunch coupons for the delay?

因為誤點，你們有提供午餐券嗎？

會話實例

例 Is the plane on schedule?

飛機會準時嗎？

例 Yes, it is.

是的。

▶ **句型 B** ◀

● The flight is an hour behind schedule.
那班飛機誤點一小時。

● Which flight are you on?
請問您搭哪一個航班呢？

● Your flight is going to be an hour late.
你的班機會延誤一小時。

會話實例

例 Can you tell me about my flight status?
你可以告訴我我的班機情況嗎？

例 Yes. Which flight are you on?
可以的，請問您搭哪一個航班呢？

例 United flight 775.
聯合 775。

例 I'll check for you, Sir. I see. Your flight
is going to be an hour late.

先生，我幫你查查看。查到了，你的班機會延誤一小時。

例 Why?

為什麼？

例 They are loading late luggage.

他們在裝晚到的行李。

 🎧 track 03-11

飛機上

Unit 11 機上入座

▶ 句型 A ◀

● Welcome aboard.

歡迎登機。

● May I see your boarding pass?

我可以看您的登機證嗎？

會話實例

例 Welcome aboard. May I see your boarding pass?

歡迎登機。我可以看您的登機證嗎？

例 Yes, of course.

好的,當然。

例 You are in aisle 22, seat A. This way, please.

您在第二十二排座位A,這邊請。

例 Thank you.

謝謝你。

▶句型 B◀

● Yes, of course.

好的,當然。

● Thank you.

謝謝你。

● Sure, here you are.

好的,在這裡。

會話實例

例 May I see your boarding pass, please?

我可以看您的登機證嗎?

例 Sure, here you are.

好的,在這裡。

例 This way, please.

這邊請。

例 Thank you.

謝謝你。

 ⌂track 03-12

Unit
12
找不到座位

▶句型 A◀

● I couldn't find my seat.
我找不到我的座位。

● Where is seat 34H?
34H在哪裡？

● Where is my seat?
我的座位在哪裡？

● Could you show me where my seat is?
你可以指出我的座位在哪嗎？

會話實例

例 Excuse me.
不好意思

例 May I help you?
需要我幫忙嗎？

例 I couldn't find my seat.
我找不到我的座位。

例 Let me see your boarding pass.

讓我看看你的登機證。

例 Here you are.

這裡。

例 Over there.

在那裡。

▶ **句型 B** ◀

● May I see your boarding pass?

我可以看你的登機證嗎？

● Go straight ahead, and you'll see it on the right side.

往前直走，你就會看到在右手邊。

● This way.

這邊請。

● It's over there, on the right aisle.

就在那裡，在右邊走道。

● It's a middle seat.

這是中間的座位。

● It's a left middle seat.

這是中間靠左的座位。

● It's a window seat on the left.

是在左邊靠窗戶的座位。

- It's an aisle seat on your right side.
  是在你的右手邊靠走道的座位。

會話實例

例 Could you tell me where my seat is?
你可以跟我說我的座位在哪嗎？

例 May I see your boarding pass?
我可以看你的登機證嗎？

 ∩track 03-13

飛機上

Unit 13

確認座位

▶句型 **A** ◀

- Is this your seat?
  這是你的坐位嗎？

- I think you are in my seat.
  我想你坐到我的位子了。

- I'm afraid this is my seat.
  這恐怕是我的座位。

- I'm afraid you have my seat.

  你恐怕坐到我的座位了。

- Someone has my seat!

  有人坐到我的坐位了！

會話實例

例 Excuse me.

不好意思。

例 Yes?

請說？

例 I'm afraid this is my seat.

這恐怕是我的座位。

例 Oh! I'm sorry.

噢！抱歉。

例 It's OK.

沒關係。

▶ 句型 B ◀

- Really? Let me check my ticket.

  真的嗎？

- Oh! I'm sorry.

  噢！抱歉。

- Oh! Sorry, my mistake.

  噢！抱歉，我坐錯了。

會話實例

例 Is this your seat?

這是你的坐位嗎？

例 Yes, I think so.

是的，我想是吧！

例 I think you are in my seat.

我想你坐到我的位子了。

例 Really? Let me check my ticket.

真的嗎？讓我確定一下。

 track 03-14

換座位

▶ 句型 A ◀

● Can I change my seat?

我可以換座位嗎？

● Is it OK if I change my seat?

我可以換座位嗎？

● Is it OK if I change my seat with you?

我可以和你換位子嗎？

● Can you switch seats with me?

我可以和你換位子嗎？

會話實例

例 Excuse me. Can I change my seat?
不好意思，我可以換座位嗎？

例 Let me see. Yes. All the passengers
are on board.
我看看。可以，所有乘客都上飛機了。

例 Is that window seat empty?
那個靠窗坐位是空的嗎？

例 Yes, it's availablc.
是的，它是空的。

▶ **句型 B** ◀

● No problem.
沒問題。

● I'm afraid not, sir.
先生，不好意思，恐怕辦不到。

● Let me see.
我看看。

會話實例

例 Excuse me. I'm in 16B. Is it OK if I
switch my seat with you?
不好意思，我坐在16B，我可以和你換位子嗎？

例 Oh, let me see. 16B, yeah, no problem.

噢，我看一下。16B，好，沒問題。

例 Thank you very much.

非常感謝你。

 ∩ track 03-15

Unit 15

放置行李

▶句型 A◀

● Can you help me put this in the overhead bin?

你可以幫我把這個放到櫃子上嗎？

● Could you help me get my bags down?

可以幫我把行李拿下來嗎？

● Would you please put this bag in the overhead bin for me?

可以你可以幫我把這個放到頭頂的置物箱嗎？

會話實例

例 Can you help me put this in the overhead bin?

你可以幫我把這個放到櫃子上嗎？

例 Sure, no problem.
好的，沒問題。

例 Thank you.
謝謝。

▶ 句型 B ◀

● May I help you?
需要我幫忙嗎？

● You can store your baggage in the over-head cabinet.
你可以把你的行李放在上方的行李櫃裡。

● No problem, madam.
沒問題，女士。

會話實例

例 May I help you?
需要我幫忙嗎？

例 Where can I put my baggage?
我要把行李放哪？

例 You can store your baggage in the overhead cabinet.
你可以把你的行李放在上方的行李櫃裡。

Unit 16 詢問廁所

▶句型A◀

- Where are the toilets?
  請問廁所在哪？

- Where is the restroom?
  洗手間在哪裡？

- How do you open the door to the bathroom?
  請問怎麼打開洗手間的門？

- Is this vacant?
  廁所是空的嗎？

會話實例

例 Excuse me?
不好意思？

例 Yes?
請說？

例 Where are the toilets?
請問廁所在哪？

例 There are two in the back.
後面有兩間。

例 Thanks!

謝謝！

▶句型 B◀

- There are two in the middle.
  中間有兩間。
- This way.
  這邊。
- Let me help you.
  我來幫你。
- This one is occupied.
  這間有人了。
- Just push the door.
  直接推門就可以了。
- It's occupied.
  廁所有人。

會話實例

例 How do you open the door to the bathroom?

請問怎麼打開洗手間的門？

例 Just push the door.

直接推門就可以了。

例 Thank you!

謝謝！

♪track 03-17

Unit 17 使用設備

▶句型A◀

● I don't have any headphones.

我沒有耳機。

● Where do I plug the headphones in?

耳機要插在哪裡？

● Where is the volume control?

音量控制在哪裡？

● Is the volume control here?

音量控制在這裡嗎？

● Can I recline my seat back now?

我可以將我的椅背往後靠嗎？

● Can I pull the arm rests up?

我可以把扶手撐起來嗎？

會話實例

例 Can I recline my seat back now?

我可以將我的椅背往後靠嗎？

例 Yes, you can.
可以的。

▶ 句型 B ◀

● Sure, here you are.
好的，給你。

● Here you go.
給你。

● Yes, you can.
可以的。

會話實例

例 I don't have any headphones.
我沒有耳機。

例 Here you go.
給你。

例 Where do I plug them in?
要插在哪裡？

例 Right here in the arm of the chair.
插在這邊，椅子的扶手上。

Unit 18
要求提供物品

▶ 句型 A ◀

● May I have a blanket?
可以請你給我一條毛毯嗎？

● Can I have another pillow?
可以再給我一個枕頭嗎？

● May I have a pack of playing cards?
可以給我一副撲克牌嗎？

● May I have a pair of earplugs?
可以給我一對耳塞嗎？

● Do you have a Chinese newspaper?
你們有中文的報紙嗎？

● Do you have any car magazines?
你們有任何汽車雜誌嗎？

會話實例

例 May I have a blanket?
可以請你給我一條毛毯嗎？

例 Sure, no problem.
好的，沒問題。

例 Thanks!

謝謝！

▶ 句型 B ◀

● Something to read?

要讀點什麼嗎？

● Sure, here you are.

好的，給你。

● Sure, no problem.

好的，沒問題。

● I'll get one for you.

我幫你拿 個。

會話實例

例 Excuse me. I'm a little cold.

不好意思，我有點冷。

例 I'll get a blanket for you.

我拿條毯子給你。

例 Can I have another pillow, too?

也可以再給我一個枕頭嗎？

例 Sure, no problem.

好的，沒問題。

機上用餐

▶句型 A◀

● What would you like for dinner, madam?
小姐,晚餐您想吃什麼呢?

● Sir, would you like chicken or fish?
先生,您要雞肉還是魚呢?

● What would you like to drink?
您要喝什麼呢?

● Tea? Does anyone want tea?
茶,有人要喝茶嗎?

● We have orange, apple and tomato juice.
我們有柳橙、蘋果跟番茄汁。

會話實例

例 Sir, would you like chicken or fish?
先生,您要雞肉還是魚呢?

例 I'd like fish.
我要魚。

例 What would you like to drink?
您要喝什麼呢?

例 Coffee, please.
請給我咖啡。

▶句型 B◀

- What do you have?
  你們有什麼？

- I'd like beef please.
  請給我牛肉。

- Do you have beer?
  你們有啤酒嗎？

- Orange juice, please.
  請給我柳橙汁。

會話實例

- What would you like to drink?
  您要喝什麼呢？

- What do you have?
  你們有什麼？

- We have orange, apple and tomato juice.
  我們有柳橙、蘋果跟番茄汁。

- Tomato juice, please.
  請給我番茄汁。

🎧track 03-20

Unit 20 詢問素食、飲料

▶句型 A◀

● Do you have a vegetarian meal?
請問有素食嗎？

● Is this a vegetarian meal?
請問有素食嗎？

● May I have another drink, please?
可以再給我一杯飲料嗎？

● May I have something to drink?
我能喝點飲料嗎？

● May I have some more coffee, please?
能再給我一點咖啡嗎？

● I'd like some sugar.
我要糖。

● Do you have any creamer?
你們有奶精嗎？

● No ice, please.
去冰，謝謝。

會話實例

例 Do you have a vegetarian meal?
請問有素食嗎？

例 Yes, I'll be right back with you.
好的，我馬上回來。

▶句型 B◀

● What would you like to drink?
您要喝什麼呢？

● How about you?
你呢？

● No problem.
沒問題。

會話實例

例 May I have another drink, please?
可以再給我一杯飲料嗎？

例 What would you like to drink?
您要喝什麼呢？

例 Apple juice, please.
請給我蘋果汁。

例 OK. How about you, madam?
好的，女士，你呢？

例 Tea, please.

請給我茶。

 🎧track 03-21

Unit 21

不舒服

▶句型 A◀

● I don't feel well.

我覺得不舒服。

● I want to vomit.

我想吐。

● I have a headache.

我頭痛。

● I have a stomachache.

我胃痛。

● I have a fever.

我發燒。

● I need medicine for air sickness.

我需要一些暈機藥。

● I'd like some medicine, please.

我需要一些藥。

會話實例

例 I want to vomit.
　　我想吐。

例 Here is an airsickness bag.
　　這裡有嘔吐袋。

例 Thanks!
　　謝謝！

▶句型 B◀

● Are you ok, sir?
　先生，你還好嗎？

● You look terrible.
　你氣色看起來不太好。

● Do you need a doctor?
　你需要醫生嗎？

● Here is an airsickness bag.
　這裡有嘔吐袋。

● Wait a moment, please.
　請等一下。

會話實例

例 Are you ok, sir?
　　先生，你還好嗎？

例 I'm not feeling well.

我覺得不舒服。

- Do you need a doctor?

你需要醫生嗎?

- Yes, I think so.

好的,我覺得需要。

- Wait a moment, please.

請等一下。

 track 03-22

Unit 22

機上買免稅商品

▶句型 **A**◀

- Our flight attendants will be coming around with the duty free cart.

我們的空服員即將過來販售免稅商品。

- Please look at the duty free catalogue located in front of you.

請參考您面前的免稅商品型錄。

- Duty free anyone?

免稅商品,有人需要嗎?

1
1
7

- Which brand do you want?
  你要哪個牌子呢？

- That will be…
  總共是…元。

會話書例

例 Duty free anyone?
  免稅商品，有人需要嗎？

例 Yes. I want to get two bottles of whis-key.
  有，我要買兩瓶威士忌。

▶ 句型 B ◀

- Do you still have this?
  你們還有這個嗎？

- I don't want this one.
  我不要這一個。

- Do you have a new one?
  你們有新的嗎？

- I'll take it.
  我要買這個。

- Where do I sign?
  我要在哪裡簽名？

3 機場與搭飛機

會話實例

例 Do you have a new one?

你們有新的嗎？

例 Yes.

有。

例 I'll take it.

那我要買這個。

例 That will be $36.

這樣是三十六美元。

Unit
23

入境卡

track 03-23

▶句型A◀

● An arrival card, please.
請給我一張入境卡。

● I need an arrival card.
我需要一張入境卡。

● May I borrow a pen?
可以借我一支筆嗎？

- What's the flight number?
  班機號碼是什麼呢？

會話實例

例 Excuse me. I need an arrival card.
我需要一張入境卡。

例 Here you are.
給你。

例 What's the flight number?
班機號碼是什麼呢？

例 It's B77201.
是 B77201。

例 Thank you.
謝謝。

▶ 句型 B ◀

- Here you are.
  給你。

- Wait a moment.
  等一下。

- I'll get one for you.
  我拿一支給你。

3 機場與搭飛機

會話實例

例 May I borrow a pen?

可以借我一支筆嗎？

例 Wait a moment. I'll get one for you.

等一下，我拿一支給你。

例 Thanks!

謝謝！

 ∩ track 03-24

Unit
24

降落

▶ **句型 A** ◀

● We are going to land soon.

我們要降落了。

● Please put your tray away.

請把你的桌子收好。

● Please return your seat to the upright position.

請把你的椅背豎直。

● Please fasten your seatbelt.

請繫上安全帶。

會話實例

例 Sir, we are going to land soon. Please put your tray away.

我們要降落了。請把你的桌子收好。

例 OK.

好的。

▶ **句型 B** ◀

● Please take this away.

請把這個收走。

● I need to put this in the overhead bin.

我要把這個放到上面的櫃子。

會話實例

例 Please fasten your seatbelt.

請繫上安全帶。

例 I need to put this in the overhead bin.

我要把這個放到上面的櫃子。

例 I'll do that for you.

我來幫你放。

● Thank you.

謝謝。

③ 機場與搭飛機

🎧 track 03-25

入境

25 轉機

▶ 句型 **A** ◀

- I have a connecting flight to New York City.
  我要轉機到紐約。

- Which gate should I go to?
  我應該要去哪一個閘門呢？

- Do I need to go to level 2?
  我要到二樓去嗎？

- Should I take the shuttle train?
  我必須搭接駁電車嗎？

- Does this transfer flight board at gate 5?
  轉機是在五號閘門登機嗎？

會話實例

例 I have a connecting flight to New York City.
我要轉機到紐約。

例 OK. Here's your boarding pass. The boarding time is 18:40. You're in 36E.
好的。這是您的登機證，登機時間是六點四十分，你的座位是36E。

例 Thank you.
謝謝。

▶ 句型 B ◀

● If you are transferring to another flight, follow the signs to the transfer area.
如果你要轉機，請順著指示牌到轉機區。

● What's your final destination?
你的最後目的地是哪呢？

● You need to report to the airline ground staff.
你要向機場地勤人員報到。

● The staff will arrange your seat for the connecting flight.
人員會幫你安排銜接班機的座位。

會話實例

例 If you are transferring to another flight, follow the signs to the transfer area.
如果你要轉機，請順著指示牌到轉機區。

例 Thank you.

謝謝。

🎧track 03-26

Unit 26

入境準備

▶句型A◀

● Which way is arrival customs?

海關在哪個方向呢？

● Which line should I get into?

我要排在哪一列？

● Is this the right place?

這地方是對的嗎？

● Is this the end of the line?

這是隊伍的盡頭嗎？

會話實例

例 Which way is arrival customs?

海關在哪個方向呢？

例 Just follow the signs.

跟著指標走。

例 Thank you.

謝謝。

▶句型**B**◀

● Just follow the signs.
跟著指標走。

● You should use the lines marked "non-residents."
你要排在標示「非本國居民」的行列。

會話實例

例 Which line should I get into?
我要排在哪一列？

例 Are you a citizen of this country?
你是這國的公民嗎？

例 No, I'm only visiting.
不，我只是來參觀的。

例 You should use the lines marked "non-residents."
你要排在標示「非本國居民」的行列。

例 I see. Thank you.
知道了，謝謝。

海關檢查

▶ 句型 **A** ◀

● May I see your passport and visa, please?

請給我看你的護照和簽證。

● What's the purpose of your visit?

你來訪的目的是什麼？

● Where will you be staying?

你要住哪裡？

● How long will you be staying in New York?

你會在紐約待多久？

● Who are you traveling with?

你跟誰一起旅行？

● What do you do?

你的職業是什麼的？

會話實例

例 What's the purpose of your visit?

你來訪的目的是什麼？

例 I'm visiting some clients.
我來拜訪一些客戶。

▶ **句型 B** ◀

● I'm on vacation.
我是來度假的。

● It's for business.
我是來出差的。

● I'm with a tour group.
我是跟旅行團來的。

● I travel by myself.
我自己旅行。

● I'm with a friend.
我跟朋友一起。

● I'll stay for 10 days.
我會停留十天。

● I'll stay at a hotel.
我住飯店。

● I'll stay with friends.
我會住朋友家。

會話實例

例 Where will you be staying?
你要住哪裡？

例 I'll stay at the Ritz hotel.

我會住在麗茲飯店。

🎧 track 03-28

Unit 28

提領行李

▶ 句型 A ◀

- Where can I get my baggage?
  請問哪裡可以提領行李？

- Where is the baggage claim area?
  行李提領區在哪？

- Could you help me get my baggage down?
  你可以幫我把行李拿下來嗎？

- That is my baggage.
  那是我的行李。

- I have nothing to claim.
  我沒有東西要申報。

- Do I have to claim this?
  我需要申報這個嗎？

會話實例

例 Do you know where baggage from Flight 207 is?

你知道班機207的行李在哪嗎？

例 Go to baggage carousel number 9.

在九號行李轉盤。

例 Thanks.

謝謝。

▶句型 B◀

● Do you have your baggage claim ticket?
你有行李單據嗎？

● Do you have anything to claim?
你有要申報什麼嗎？

● May I see your baggage claim ticket?
請給我看你的行李單據。

會話實例

例 Do you have anything to claim?
你有要申報什麼嗎？

例 No, I don't.
沒有。

例 OK then. Please pass through the arrival gate.

好的，那請從入境門過去。

3 機場與搭飛機

🎧 track 03-29

Unit 29 遺失行李

▶ 句型 A ◀

- I can't find my baggage.
  我找不到我的行李。

- My baggage is not here.
  我的行李不在這裡。

- One of my bags hasn't come.
  我有一件行李沒有出來。

- I think I've lost my baggage.
  我想我的行李遺失了。

- We may have lost some baggage.
  我們可能遺失一些行李了。

- Where is The Lost Luggage Service?
  行李遺失服務處在哪裡呢？

會話實例

例 I think I've lost my baggage.
  我想我的行李遺失了。

例 Please tell me the flight you were on.
  請告訴我你搭幾號班機。

例 Flight 553 from Taipei.

從台北出發的553班機。

例 I see. I'll tell the baggage handlers to look for it.

我知道了，我會告訴行李人員尋找你的行李。

▶句型B◀

- Please tell me the flight you were on.
  請告訴我你搭幾號班機。

- How many bags are missing?
  你少了幾個袋子？

- Can you tell me the features of your baggage?
  你可以描述一下你的行李外觀嗎？

- Please fill this claim form in.
  請填寫這張申訴表格。

會話實例

例 Can you tell me the features of your baggage?

你可以描述一下你的行李外觀嗎？

例 It's red and with wheels.

是紅色有輪子的。

3 機場與搭飛機

例 OK, let me check.

好的，我確認一下。

例 This one?

這個嗎？

例 Yes, thank you very much.

非常感謝你！

🎧 track 03-30

Unit 30

兌換錢幣

▶句型A◀

- Where is the Currency Exchange?

「錢幣兌換處」在哪裡？

- Where can I exchange money?

請問哪裡可以兌換錢幣？

- I'd like to exchange money.

我想要兌換錢幣。

- I want to exchange for U.S. dollars.

我要換美金。

- What's the exchange rate?

請問匯率是多少？

- Could you break this bill?

你可以將這張紙鈔換成零錢嗎？

- I'd like to change NT$ 10,000 into U. S. dollars.
  我要把一萬元台幣換成美金。

會話實例

例 Where can I exchange money?
請問哪裡可以兌換錢幣？

例 It's over there.
在那裡。

▶句型 B◀

- How much would you like to change?
  要換成多少？
- What are you exchanging?
  要用什麼貨幣換？
- Today's rates are shown here.
  今天的匯率顯示在這邊。

會話實例

例 What's the exchange rate?
請問匯率是多少？

例 Today's rates are shown here.
今天的匯率顯示在這邊。

例 I see. Thank you.
知道了，謝謝。

3 機場與搭飛機

🎧 track 03-31

你一定要聽懂的10句話

1. May I help you?
   有什麼需要我效勞的嗎？

2. May I see your passport and visa, please?
   請給我看你的護照和簽證。

3. Sure, no problem.
   好的，沒問題。

4. Here you are.
   給你。

5. What would you like for dinner, madam?
   小姐，晚餐您想吃什麼呢？

6. Sir, would you like chicken or fish?
   先生，您要雞肉還是魚呢？

7. What would you like to drink?
   您要喝什麼呢？

8. I'll be right back with you.
   我馬上回來。

9. Please fasten your seatbelt.
   請繫上安全帶。

10. What's the purpose of your visit?
    你來訪的目的是什麼？

● 1
● 3
● 5

你一定要會說的 10 句話

1. I'd like to make a flight reservation.
   我要預約機位。
2. Check-in, please.
   我要辦理登機。
3. Where is the boarding gate?
   登機門在哪裡？
4. I couldn't find my seat.
   我找不到我的座位。
5. Can you help me put this in the overhead bin?
   你可以幫我把這個放到櫃子上嗎？
6. Where are the toilets?
   請問廁所在哪？
7. May I have a blanket?
   可以請你給我一條毛毯嗎？
8. I don't feel well.
   我覺得不舒服。
9. I have a connecting flight to New York City.
   我要轉機到紐約。
10. Which way is arrival customs?
    海關在哪個方向呢？

3 機場與搭飛機

Chapter

4

問路與交通

問路

Unit 1 目的地

▶句型A◀

- How can I get to Times Square?
  我要怎麼去時代廣場？

- Do you know where the post office is?
  你知道郵局在哪裡嗎？

- I'd like to go to Brooklyn Bridge.
  我要去布魯克林大橋。

- I'm going to Manhattan.
  我要去曼哈頓。

- Do I have to change buses?
  我應該要換公車嗎？

- Can I get there by bus?
  我可以搭公車去嗎？

- Which direction, please?
  哪個方向？

❹ 問路與交通

就是這一本超實用的
旅遊英語

會話實例

例 Do you know where the post office is?
你知道郵局在哪裡嗎？

例 It's next to the school.
在學校旁邊。

例 Thank you.
謝謝。

▶句型 B◀

● You can take bus number 17.
你可以搭十七路公車。

● You can get there by transit.
你可以搭交通工具過去。

● You can get there by subway.
你可以搭地鐵過去。

● You can go there by walking.
你可以走路過去。

● That way.
那個方向。

會話實例

例 Excuse me. How can I get to Times Square?
不好意思。我要怎麼去時代廣場？

138

例 You can take bus number 17.
你可以搭十七路公車。

例 Thank you.
謝謝。

🎧 track 04-02

Unit
2
步行

▶句型A◀

● How to get there on foot?
用步行的要如何到那裡？

● Can I get there on foot?
我可以走路過去嗎？

會話實例

例 Excuse me. Where is the nearest supermarket?
不好意思，請問最近的超市在哪裡？

例 That way.
那個方向。

例 Can I get there on foot?
我可以走路過去嗎？

例 Yes. Just go straight ahead.

可以，只要直走就可以了。

例 Thank you.

謝謝。

▶句型 B◀

- You can get there on foot.
  你可以走路過去。

- You could walk if you would like.
  你想要的話，可以用走的過去。

- Just go straight ahead.
  只要直走就可以了。

會話實例

例 Excuse me. Where is the train station?
不好意思，火車站在哪裡？

例 That way, go straight.
往那個方向直走。

例 Is it far from here?
會很遠嗎？

例 You could walk if you would like.
你想要的話，可以用走的過去。

例 I got it. Thanks.
我知道了，謝謝！

track 04-03

Unit 3 距離

▶句型A◀

● How far is it?
有多遠?

● How far is it from here?
距離這裡有多遠?

● Is the Metropolitan Museum of Art close to here?
紐約大都會博物館離這裡近嗎?

● How close are we to Philadelphia?
我們離費城有多近?

● Is it far?
會很遠嗎?

會話實例

例 How about going to Central Park?
要不要去中央公園?

例 How far is it?
有多遠?

例 It's about 500 meters.

大約五百公尺。

例 OK.

好啊。

▶句型 B◀

- It's about 10 miles.
  大約有十公里。

- It's quite far away.
  有點遠。

- It's a long distance.
  距離很遠。

- It's just 5 minutes' walk from here.
  從這裡只有五分鐘的步行路程。

會話實例

例 Would you like to go to Navy Pier?

你想去海軍碼頭嗎？

例 Is it far?

會很遠嗎？

例 It's just 5 minutes' walk from here.

從這裡只有五分鐘的步行路程。

例 OK.

好啊。

例 Let's go.
走吧。

track 04-04

公車/巴士

購票

►句型A◄

- Where can I buy the tickets?
  哪裡可以買車票?

- I'd like to buy a ticket to Buffalo, please.
  我要買一張到水牛城的車票。

- How much is the ticket to Dallas?
  到達拉斯的票要多少錢?

- An adult to Nice, please.
  一張到尼斯的成人票。

- Here you are.
  給你。

會話實例

例 I'd like to buy a ticket to Buffalo, please.

我要買一張到水牛城的車票。

例 Here you are.

給你。

▶句型 B◀

- It's on the corner.

就在那個角落。

- The bus to Dallas costs $30.

到達拉斯的巴士要三十美元。

會話實例

例 Where can I buy the tickets?

哪裡可以買車票？

例 It's on the corner.

就在那個角落。

例 Thanks.

謝啦！

Unit 5 搭哪一班公車

▶句型A◀

● Where is the bus station?
公車站在哪裡？

● Which bus could I get on to the airport?
哪班公車有到機場呢？

● Do you know which way that is on?
你知道我該做哪一線嗎？

● Could you tell me how to find bus 7?
你可以告訴我七號公車在哪搭嗎？

● Which way is it to East Village?
哪個方向是往東村？

● Where can I transfer to No. 8?
我可以在哪轉乘八號公車呢？

● Where does the bus to Woodbury Outlet depart from?
開往伍德柏里賣場的公車從哪裡發車呢？

4 問路與交通

會話實例

例 Which bus could I get on to the airport?
哪班公車有到機場呢？

例 You can take bus number 18.
你可以搭十八路公車。

例 Thanks.
謝謝！

▶**句型 B**◀

● Turn right and you will see the bus station.
右轉你就會看到公車站。

● You can take the 407 or 503.
你可以搭407或503。

● Go across the street and walk that way.
穿過街道往那邊走。

會話實例

例 Where can I transfer to No. 8?
我可以在哪轉乘八號公車呢？

例 Go across the street and walk that way.
穿過街道往那邊走。

例 Thank you.
謝謝。

🎧 track 04-06

Unit 6
公車的目的地

▶句型A◀

- Does this bus go to Cambridge University?

  這班公車有到劍橋大學嗎？

- Is this the right bus to the Empire State Building?

  這是去帝國大廈的公車嗎？

- Is this the bus to downtown?

  這是去市區的公車嗎？

- Does this bus stop at City Hall?

  這班公車有停市政府那站嗎？

- Where can I catch the bus to Central Park?

  哪裡有開往中央公園的公車？

會話書例

例 Does this bus stop at City Hall?

這班公車有停市政府那站嗎？

❹ 問路與交通

例 Yes, it stops at City Hall.

有，有到市政府。

▶句型 B◀

- Yes, it goes to City Hall.

  有，有到市政府。

- Yes, it is.

  是的。

- No, you have to take bus 606.

  沒有，你要搭606號公車。

- No, you have to go across the street.

  沒有，你必須到對面去搭。

會話實例

例 Does this bus go to Cambridge University?

這班公車有到劍橋大學嗎？

例 Yes, it goes to Cambridge University.

有，有到劍橋大學。

在哪下車

▶句型A◀

- Where is the next bus station?
  下一站公車站是哪裡？

- Where can I get off?
  我該在哪裡下車？

- Where should I get off?
  我應該在哪裡下車？

- Please tell me when to get off.
  請告訴我何時要下車。

- What's the name of the bus stop before I get off?
  我下車的前一站是什麼？

- Let me off here, please.
  我要在這裡下車。

- Here comes my bus.
  我的公車來了。

會話實例

例 Is this the Four Seasons Hotel?
這是四季飯店嗎？

❹ 問路與交通

例 Yes, it is.

是的。

例 Let me off here, please.

我要在這裡下車。

例 Sure.

好的。

▶句型B◀

● May I help you?

需要我的協助嗎?

● Where are you going?

你要去哪裡?

● No problem.

沒問題。

會話實例

例 May I help you?

需要我的協助嗎?

例 We're going to Yankee Stadium. Please tell us when to get off.

我們要去洋基體育場,請告訴我們何時要下車。

例 No problem.

沒問題。

例 Thank you.
謝謝。

track 04-08

Unit 8 車程及站數

▶句型A◀

- How long is the ride?
  這趟車程要多久?

- How long will the ride take?
  要搭多久的車呢?

- How long is the trip?
  這趟車程要多久?

- How long will it be before we stop by the next rest area?
  到下一個休息區還要多久?

- When will I reach Chicago?
  我何時會到芝加哥?

- How many stops are there from here?
  離這裡有幾站?

④ 問路與交通

● How many stops are there to the market?
市場離這裡有幾站？

會話實例

例 How long is the ride?
這趟車程要多久？

例 It'll take about 3 hours.
大約會需要三小時。

►句型 B◄

● It's about 30 minutes.
大約三十分鐘。

● It'll take about 2 hours.
大約會需要兩小時。

● It usually takes 50 minutes to get there.
通常需要五十分鐘才能到那裡。

會話實例

例 How many stops are there to the market?
市場離這裡有幾站？

例 That's the fourth stop.
那是第四個站。

例 Please tell me when to get off.
請告訴我何時要下車。

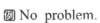
例 No problem.
沒問題。

例 Thank you.
謝謝。

 track 04-09

發車頻率及時間

▶句型A◀

● How often does this bus run?
這班公車多久來一班呢？

● How often does this bus come?
公車多久來一班呢？

● When will the bus depart?
公車何時出發？

會話實例

例 How often does this bus run?
這班公車多久來一班呢？

例 It comes about every 10 minutes.
大概每十分鐘來一班。

❹
問路與交通

例 Great.

太好了。

例 There's one coming now.

有一班來了。

例 Thank you.

謝謝。

▶句型B◀

- It comes about every 5 minutes.

  大概每五分鐘來一班。

- About 20 minutes.

  大約二十分鐘。

- It'll depart at 10:00 am.

  早上十點發車。

- It starts out at 8 am.

  早上八點就開車了。

會話實例

例 When will the bus depart?

公車何時出發？

例 It starts out at 8 am.

早上八點就開車了。

例 Oh, thanks. I gotta go now.

噢，謝謝。我該走了。

火車站

購票

▸句型A◂

- I need one ticket to Lyon.
  我要一張到里昂的車票。

- How much does it cost to Los Angeles?
  到洛杉磯一張車票多少錢？

- I'd like a one-way ticket to New York, please.
  我要買一張到紐約單程車票。

- How much is the ticket from Strasbourg to Paris?
  從史特拉斯堡到巴黎的票價是多少？

- Can I use a credit card to pay for the ticket?
  我可以用信用卡付票錢嗎？

會話實例

例 I need one ticket to Seattle.

我要一張到西雅圖的車票。

例 That's a three day trip. Do you want a sleeper?

那是個三天的旅程,你要臥鋪嗎?

例 How much does it cost?

要多少錢呢?

例 $225 one way.

單趟225元。

▶句型B◀

● Yes, you can.

是的,你可以。

● One way for $1490.

單程1490元。

● The ticket from Boston to New York is $69.

從波士頓到紐約的票是69美元。

● Do you want a sleeper?

你要臥鋪嗎?

會話實例

例 How much is the ticket from Strasbourg to Paris?

從史特拉斯堡到巴黎的票價是多少？

例 One way for €69.

單程六十九歐元。

 ∩ track 04-11

搭車月台

▶句型A◀

● Which platform is it on?
在哪一個月台？

● Is this the right platform for Buffalo?
這是出發到水牛城的月台嗎？

● Is this the right train for downtown?
這是去市中心的火車嗎？

● Where should I get on the train?
我應該要在哪上車？

● Which train goes to Buffalo?
哪一班車到水牛城？

- Which line should I take to Buffalo?
  我應該搭哪一線去水牛城？

- Which train can I take to buffalo?
  我要去水牛城應該要搭哪一班車？

會話舉例

例 Which platform is it on?
在哪一個月台？

例 It's on the 4th platform.
在第四月台。

例 I see. Thank you.
我知道了，謝謝。

▶句型 B◀

- It's on the 2nd platform.
  在第二月台。

- You can check the map over there.
  你可以查在那裏的地圖。

- Is this the platform for Lyon?
  這是出發到里昂的月台？

- This train goes to Nante.
  這一班車到南特。

會話舉例

例 Which line should I take to Buffalo?
我應該搭哪一線去水牛城？

例 You can check the map over there.
你可以查在那裏的地圖。

🎧 track 04-12

行李寄放

▶句型A◀

● Where is the baggage room?
請問行李寄放處在哪？

● Can I store baggage here?
我可以在這寄放行裡嗎？

● I need to store luggage.
我要寄放行李。

● I need to store these two bags for three days.
我要把這兩個袋子寄放三天。

● What time does the baggage storage open/close?
行李寄放處幾點開／關門？

● I want to pick up my stored luggage.
我要領回我寄放的行李。

● What are your shop hours?
請問你們的營業時間是幾點？

會話實例

例 I need to store this bag for three days.
我要把這個袋子寄放三天。

例 OK. I need to see your ID, please.
好的，請給我看你的證件，謝謝。

例 Is my passport good enough?
護照可以嗎？

例 Sure.
當然。

▶句型B◀

● The charge per day is $7.
每日收費是七元。

● Let me see your number tag, please.
請讓我看你的號碼牌。

● I need to see your ID, please.
請給我看你的證件，謝謝。

● You need to sign this agreement.
你要簽這份同意書。

- You have to keep this number tag.
  你要留著這個號碼牌。

- The baggage storage is open from 7:00 am to 22:00 pm.
  行李寄放處從早上七點開到晚上十點。

會話實例

例 I want to claim my stored bags.
  我要領回我寄放的袋子。

例 Let me see your number tag, please.
  請讓我看你的號碼牌。

 🎧 track 04-13

地鐵

Unit 13 搭地鐵、捷運

▶句型A◀

- Is there a subway station nearby?
  附近有地鐵站嗎？

- Is there a MRT nearby?
  附近有捷運站嗎？

- Where can I buy a ticket?
  哪裡可以買票呢？

- Where can I buy a mass transit card?
  哪裡可以買大眾運輸卡呢？

- I'd like to buy a MetroCard.
  我要買一張捷運卡。

- Can you show me how to use the ticket machine?
  你可以教我怎麼使用售票機嗎？

- Which side of the platform goes north?
  請問月台的哪一側是往北？

會話實例

例 Where can I buy a mass transit card?
哪裡可以買大眾運輸卡呢？

例 At that booth over there.
在那邊那個亭子。

例 Thank you.
謝謝。

▶句型 B◀

- You need to go to the other side.
  你要到另一邊去。

- You'll need to transfer after two stops.
  你要在兩站後轉車。

- How many days do you need?
  你需要幾天的？

- There is a subway station nearby.
  附近有地鐵站。

- You can buy tickets at that booth.
  你可以在那個亭子買票。

會話實例

例 I'd like to buy a mass transit system card.
  我要買一張大眾運輸卡。

例 OK. We have different kinds. How
  many days do you need?
  好的，我們有不同種類，你需要幾天的？

例 Five days.
  五天的。

❹
問路與交通

track 04-14

計程車

Unit 14
告知目的地

►句型**A**◄

- Are you in service?
  你現在有服務嗎？

- Is this taxi metered?
  這計程車是跳表的嗎？

- What's the flat rate?
  起跳多少錢？

- Please take me to this address.
  請載我到這個地址。

- Please to this place.
  請到這個地方。

- Please take me to the Metropolitan Museum of Art.
  請送我到紐約大都會博物館。

- City hall, please.
  請到市政府。

會話實例

例 Are you in service?
你現在有服務嗎?

例 Yes, I am. Where to?
是的。你要去哪裡?

例 Please take me to the Rockefeller Center.
請送我到洛克斐勒中心。

▶句型 B◀

● Are you looking for a taxi?
需要搭計程車嗎?

● Where to?
你要去哪裡?

● Where would you like to go?
你要去哪裡?

● No problem.
沒問題。

● Please fasten your seatbelt.
請繫安全帶。

會話實例

例 Where would you like to go?
你要去哪裡?

例 Please take me to the airport.
請送我到機場。

例 No problem.
沒問題。

🎧 track 04-15

Unit 15

盡速抵達

▶句型A◀

● Could you drive faster?
你可以開快一點嗎？

● I'm in a hurry.
我趕時間。

● Please get us there quickly.
請趕快載我們到那邊。

● How much would it cost to drive two people around the city all day?
請問兩人一起包車市內遊覽整天要多少錢？

會話實例

例 We're late for a show. Please get us there quickly.
我們看秀遲到了，請趕快載我們到那邊。

166

- Certainly.
  沒問題。

▶句型 B◀

- No problem.
  沒問題。

- I'll take one for \$100, two for \$150.
  我載一位乘客收費一百元，兩位一百五十元。

- What time do you want me to pick you up?
  你要我幾點來接你？

會話實例

例 How much would it cost to drive two people around the city all day?
請問兩人一起包車市內遊覽整天要多少錢？

例 Two for \$150.
兩位一百五十元

例 It's a good price.
這是個好價錢。

例 I don't want to do it today, but tomorrow.
我不想今天遊市區，要明天。

例 No problem. What time do you want me to pick you up?

沒問題。你要我幾點來接你？

例 9 o'clock at this hotel.

九點在這個旅館。

track 04-16

Unit 16 下車

▶句型A◀

● Let me off at the traffic light.

讓我在紅綠燈處下車。

● Just drop me off at the next corner.

下一個轉彎讓我下車就行了。

● Let me off at the third building.

讓我在第三棟大樓前下車。

● How much is the fare?

多少錢？

● How much?

多少錢？

● Keep the change.

不用找零了。

會話實例

例 Let me off at the traffic light.
讓我在紅綠燈處下車。

例 Yes, sir. Here you are.
好的，先生，到了。

▶**句型 B**◀

● Here you are.
到了。

會話實例

例 How much is the fare?
多少錢？

例 Two hundred and fifty dollars.
兩百五十元。

例 Here you are. Keep the change.
給你，不用找零了。

例 Thank you, sir.
謝謝你，先生。

4
問路與交通

track 04-17

租車

Unit 17 預約、租車

►句型A◄

- I'd like to reserve a van.
  我要預約一輛休旅車。
- I'd like to reserve a Toyota for a week.
  我要預約一個星期的豐田的車。
- I'd like to rent a car.
  我要租車。
- I'd like to rent this car for a week.
  我要租這輛車一個星期的時間。
- I'll need it from this Monday to Friday.
  我這個星期一到星期五會用到這輛車。
- Could I have one for tomorrow morning?
  我明天早上就能用車嗎？

會話實例

例 I'd like to rent a car.
我要租車。

例 What kind of car do you want?
你要什麼樣的車？

例 I'd like a mid-size sedan.
我要中型轎車。

▶句型 B◀

● Do you have a reservation?
你有預約嗎？

● What can I do for you?
你需要什麼服務？

● When do you want the car?
你什麼時候要用車。

會話實例

例 I'd like a BMW.
我要BMW的車。

例 OK, please fill in this form. When do
you want the car?
好的，填這個表格。你什麼時候要用車？

4
問路與交通

例 I'll take it right now, if possible.

如果可以的話,我現在就要。

🎧 track 04-18

Unit 18

種類、還車地點

▶句型A◀

- I'd like some information about renting a car.

  我想要知道一些租車的資訊。

- What kinds of cars do you have available?

  你們有什麼樣的車可以租呢?

- How old are your cars?

  你們的車多老呢?

- Can I drop it off in a different city?

  我可以在另一個城市還嗎?

- Can I leave the car at any agency?

  我可以在其他車行還車嗎?

- Do I have to return the car here?

  我要回到這裡還車嗎?

會話實例

例 I'd like some information about renting a car.

我想要知道一些租車的資訊。

例 What do you want to know?

你想要知道什麼？

例 What kinds of cars do you have available?

你們有什麼樣的車可以租呢？

▶句型 B◀

- What kind of car do you want?
  你要什麼樣的車？

- Which car would you like?
  你要哪一種車？

- You may return it to our branches anywhere.
  你可以在我們任何一家分公司還車。

- You don't have to return the car here.
  你不需要回到這裡還車。

❹ 問路與交通

會話實例

例 I'd like a Buick.
我要別克的車。

例 OK. Please fill in this form.
　好的，請填這個表格。

例 Do I have to return the car here?
　我要回到這裡還車嗎？

例 No. You may return it to our branches anywhere.
　不用，你可以在我們任何一家分公司還車。

◯ track 04-19

Unit
19
租車費用

►句型 A◄

● What's the rate for a car?
　租一輛車要多少錢？

● How much is it to rent a car?
　租一輛車要多少錢？

● I want to rent a van, how much would it cost?
　我想要租一輛休旅車，要多少錢？

● How much does it cost to rent a car?
　租一輛車要多少錢？

- What's the weekly rate for a car?
  租一星期要多少？

- Does this price include insurance?
  這個價格有包含保險嗎？

- What does this insurance cover?
  這個保險包括哪些？

會話實例

例 What's the rate for a car?
  租一輛車要多少錢？

例 The daily rate is $60.
  每天的租金是六十美金。

▶句型B◀

- The daily rate is $50.
  每天的租金是五十美金。

- It's $200 a week.
  一星期要兩百美元。

- This price includes insurance.
  這個價格有包含保險。

會話實例

例 How much is it to rent a car?
  租一輛車要多少錢？

例 The daily rate is $60.
每天的租金是六十美金。

例 Does this price include full insurance?
這個價格有包含全險嗎？

例 Of course.
當然有。

Unit
20
填寫資料

▶句型A◀

● Here's my international driver's license.
這是我的國際駕照。

● Here's my ID.
這是我的證件。

會話書例

例 Your driver's license, please.
請給我你的駕照。

例 Sure. Here's my international driver's license.
好的，這是我的國際駕照。

例 And your credit card, please.
還有你的信用卡。

例 Here you are.
給你。

▶句型 **B**◀

● Your driver's license, please.
請給我你的駕照。

● May I see your driver's license?
可以給我看你的駕照嗎？

● Do you have your driver's license?
你有帶駕照嗎？

● I need your driver's license and credit card.
我需要你的駕照跟信用卡。

● OK, please fill in this form.
好的，請填寫這張表格。

● Complete this form and sign your name at the bottom.
填寫這份表格，然後在最下面簽名。

會話實例

例 I have a reservation.
我有預約。

例 I need your driver's license and credit card.

我需要你的駕照跟信用卡。

例 Here you are.

給你。

例 OK, please fill in this form.

好的,請填寫這張表格。

 ⌾ track 04-21

(Unit 21)

索取地圖、加油

▶句型A◀

● May I have a map of this city?
可以給我一份城市地圖嗎?

● Is there a gas station nearby?
請問附近有加油站嗎?

● Fill'er up, please.
請加滿。

● Could you fill'er up with supreme?
請加滿高級汽油。

● Fill'er up with regular.
普通汽油加滿。

- Twenty dollars worth, please.
  請加二十元的汽油。

- What type of gas would you recommend for this car?
  可以幫我看這輛車該加什麼油嗎？

會話實例

例 Could you fill'er up with supreme?
請加滿高級汽油。

例 Sure.
沒問題。

▶句型 B◀

- Cash or charge?
  付現還是刷卡？

- Cash or credit?
  付現還是刷卡？

會話實例

例 Fill'er up, please.
請加滿。

例 Cash or charge?
付現還是刷卡？

例 I'll charge it.
我要刷卡。

● OK, it came to \$26.75. Just a second.
好的,總共是26.75元,稍等一下。

● Thanks.
謝謝。

track 04-22

Unit
22
收費公路、停車

▶句型A◀

● I need toll tickets.
我要回數票。

● I need a toll road pass.
我要收費公路通行卡。

● I'd like to buy a book of toll tickets.
我要買一本回數票。

● What amounts are they available in?
可以有多少金額的呢?

● I want to park here.
我想在這裡停車。

● How do we pay?
我們要怎麼付費呢？

【會話實例】

例 I'd like to buy a book of toll tickets.
我要買一本回數票。

例 We only sell pass cards.
我們只有賣通行卡。

例 What amounts are they available in?
可以有多少金額的呢？

例 Thirty dollars is the cheapest.
三十元是最便宜的。

▶句型B◀

● Do you need a toll road pass?
你需要收費公路通行卡嗎？

● You can park in any empty spot.
你可以停在任何空位。

● Pay the cashier at the exit when you leave.
離開時在出口付給收費員。

【會話實例】

例 I want to park here.
我想在這裡停車。

- You can park in any empty spot.
  你可以停在任何空位。

Unit
23

🎧track 04-23

警察攔停

▶句型A◀

- May I see your driver's license?
  我可以看你的駕照嗎？

- Do you have the registration for this car?
  你有行照嗎？

- I'm going to give you a verbal warning this time.
  我只給你口頭警告。

- I suggest you check out the local driving regulations.
  我建議你注意本地的開車規定。

- Drive carefully.
  小心駕駛。

會話實例

例 May I see your driver's license?
  我可以看你的駕照嗎？

例 Here it is, officer.

在這裡，警察先生。

► 句型 B ◄

● Here's my license.

這是我的駕照。

● May I ask what the problem is?

我可以知道是什麼問題嗎？

● Did I do something wrong, officer?

警察先生，我做錯什麼了嗎？

● I didn't know it's not all right.

我不知道那樣不行。

● Is that illegal?

那是違法的嗎？

會話實例

例 Did I do something wrong, officer?

警察先生，我做錯什麼了嗎？

例 You passed a car while crossing the bridge.

你剛剛過橋時超車。

例 Sorry, officer. I'll be more careful from now on.

抱歉，警察先生，我現在起會更小心。

🎧 track 04-24

車子故障

▶句型A◀

- I don't know if you can help me.
  不知道你可以幫我嗎？

- My car's broken down.
  我的車壞了

- My car won't start.
  我的車發不動。

- It won't start.
  沒辦法發動。

- I have a flat tire.
  我的輪胎沒氣了。

會話實例

例 Do you need help?
你需要幫忙嗎？

例 My car won't start.
我的車發不動。

例 I'll see what I can do. You've just run out of gas.
我來看看能幫什麼忙。你車子沒油啦！

▶句型 B◀

- What happened?
  發生什麼事了？

- What happened to your car?
  你的車怎麼了？

- Where are you?
  你在哪裡？

- I'll see what I can do.
  我看看能幫什麼忙。

- I'll send a mechanic out to you.
  我會派技工過去你那裡。

- I'll call a tow truck for you.
  我幫你叫一輛拖車。

會話實例

例 What happened?
  發生什麼事了？

例 My car broke down on the freeway.
  我的車在高速公路上拋錨了。

例 I'll call a tow truck for you.
  我幫你叫一輛拖車。

例 I really appreciate it.
  太感謝了！

你一定要聽懂的 10 句話

1. That way.
   那個方向。
2. You can get there on foot.
   你可以走路過去。
3. You can take the 407 or 503.
   你可以搭 407 或 503。
4. You can check the map over there.
   你可以查在那裏的地圖。
5. Let me see your number tag, please.
   請讓我看你的號碼牌。
6. Where would you like to go?
   你要去哪裡？
7. What kind of car do you want?
   你要什麼樣的車？
8. May I see your driver's license?
   可以給我看你的駕照嗎？
9. Complete this form and sign your name at the bottom.
   填寫這份表格，然後在最下面簽名。
10. Cash or charge?
    付現還是刷卡？

你一定要會說的 10 句話

1. How can I get to Times Square?
   我要怎麼去時代廣場？

2. How far is it?
   有多遠？

3. Where can I buy the tickets?
   哪裡可以買車票？

4. Which bus could I get on to the airport?
   哪班公車有到機場呢？

5. Let me off here, please.
   我要在這裡下車。

6. How long is the ride?
   這趟車程要多久？

7. I'd like a one-way ticket to New York, please.
   我要買一張到紐約單程車票。

8. Is this the right platform to Buffalo?
   這是出發到水牛城的月台嗎？

9. I'd like to rent a car.
   我要租車。

10. May I have a map of this city?
    可以給我一份城市地圖嗎？

Chapter

5

郵寄及電話用語

track 05-01

撥電話找人

▶句型A◀

- May I speak to John?
  我能跟約翰講電話嗎？

- Can I talk to Karen, please?
  我可以跟凱倫講電話嗎？

- Could I talk to Ernie or William?
  我可以跟爾尼或威廉講電話嗎？

- Is Amy there?
  艾咪在嗎？

- I need to talk to Johnson.
  我要和強生通電話。

- Is this Steven speaking?
  你是史帝文嗎？

- This is Alicia calling Bruce.
  我是艾莉西亞，我要找布魯斯。

會話實例

例 May I speak to Peter?
我能跟彼得講電話嗎？

例 Speaking.

我就是，請説。

▶句型 B◀

● Speaking.

我就是，請説。

● May I help you?

需要我效勞嗎？

● Let me take a look.

我看一下。

● I can't talk to you now.

我現在不方便講電話。

會話實例

例 May I speak to John?

我能跟約翰講電話嗎？

例 Who is calling, please?

你是哪一位？

例 This is Miranda.

我是米蘭達。

例 OK. I'll put you through.

好的，我幫你轉接。

🎧track 05-02

詢問來電者身分

▶句型A◀

- Who is calling, please?
  你是哪一位？

- Who is this?
  請問哪裡找？

- May I have your name, please?
  請問您的大名？

- May I ask who is calling?
  請問您的大名？

- Who should I say is calling?
  我要說是誰來電？

- And you are?
  那麼你是？

- Are you Mr. Smith?
  你是史密斯先生嗎？

會話書例

例 May I ask who is calling?
請問您的大名？

例 This is Winnie.

我是維妮。

►句型 B ◄

● This is Andy.

我是安迪。

● This is Bob Johnson.

我是鮑伯強生。

會話實例

例 May I speak to Mr. Jones?

我可以和瓊斯先生講話嗎？

例 Who is calling, please?

你是哪一位？

例 This is Andy.

我是安迪。

例 Please wait a moment.

請等一下。

請稍候

▶句型A◀

- Is Jack around?
  傑克在嗎？

- Is Becky in the office now?
  貝琪現在在辦公室嗎？

- When will he be back?
  他什麼時候會回來？

會話實例

例 Hi, Cindy? This is Henry.
嗨，辛蒂？我是亨利。

例 Hi, Henry. How are you doing?
嗨，亨利。你好嗎？

例 Great. Is Allen around?
很好，亞倫在嗎？

例 Yes, he is. Hold on, please.
是的，他在。請等一下。

❺ 郵寄及電話用語

▶句型 B◀

- Hold on, please.
  請等一下。

- Hang on, please.
  請等一下。

- Wait a moment.
  等一下。

- Just a minute, please.
  請等一下。

- Hold the line, please.
  請稍等不要掛斷電話。

- Would you wait a moment, please?
  能請你稍等一下嗎？

- Would you mind holding for one minute?
  你介意稍等一下嗎？

- Sorry to have kept you waiting.
  不好意思讓你等那麼久。

會話實例

例 Would you wait a moment, please?
能請你稍等一下嗎？

194

例 OK. Thank you.

好的，謝謝。

track 05-04

Unit 4

代接電話

▶**句型A**◀

- Would you tell him to answer my call?

  你可以請他接我電話嗎？

- Can I call again in 10 minutes?

  我可以十分鐘後再打過來嗎？

會話實例

例 Is Carmen around?

卡門在嗎？

例 Let me see if she is in.

我看看她在不在。

例 Thank you.

謝謝。

例 She's still on the phone.

她還在講電話。

例 Can I call again in 10 minutes?
我可以十分鐘後再打過來嗎？

▶句型B◀

- Let me see if he is in.
  我看看他在不在。

- Let me scc if he is available.
  我看看他有沒有空。

- He's still on the phone.
  他還在講電話。

- He's on another line.
  他在忙線中。

- He's in a meeting now.
  他正在開會中。

- You can try again in a few minutes.
  你可以過幾分鐘再打來看看。

- He's out to lunch.
  他外出去吃午餐。

會話實例

例 Is Mark there?
馬克在嗎？

例 He's on another line.
他在忙線中。

- OK. I see. I'll try again in a few minutes.
  好的，我知道了。我過幾分鐘再打來看看。

🎧track 05-05

Unit 5
電話留言

▶句型A◀

- May I leave a message?
  我可以留言嗎？

- Could I leave him a message?
  我可以留言給他嗎？

- Please tell her I called.
  請轉告她我有打電話來。

- Would you tell him I called?
  可以請你幫我轉告他我來電過嗎？

- Please ask him to call me back.
  請告訴他回我電話。

- Please tell him to return my call.
  請告訴他回我電話。

- Tell him to give me a call as soon as possible.
  請他盡快回我電話。

會話實例

例 May I leave a message?

我可以留言嗎？

例 Sure.

當然。

例 Please tell him to return my call.

請告訴他回我電話。

▶句型 B◀

● Would you like to leave a message?

你要留言嗎？

● May I take a message?

要我記下留言嗎？

● What do you want me to tell him?

要我轉達什麼給他嗎？

● Do you have any message?

你有要留言嗎？

● Let me take a message.

我來記下留言。

● Let me write down your message.

我來寫下你的留言。

● Do you want him to return your call?

你要他回你電話嗎？

- Does he have your phone number?
  他知道你的電話號碼嗎？

會話實例

例 Would you like to leave a message?
  你要留言嗎？

例 Please tell her Jin called.
  請轉告她琴有打電話來。

 🎧 track 05-06

Unit 6

打錯電話

► 句型 A ◄

- Do I have the wrong number?
  我打錯電話號碼了嗎？

- I'm calling 1-125-782-9099.
  我打 1-125-782-9099。

會話實例

例 Do I have the wrong number?
  我打錯電話號碼了嗎？

例 What number are you dialing?
  你打幾號？

❺ 郵寄及電話用語

- I'm calling 1-205-309-8547.
  我打 1-205-309-8547

- You have the wrong number.
  你撥錯電話號碼了。

- Oh. I'm sorry.
  噢，真不好意思。

▶句型 B◀

- You must have the wrong number.
  你一定撥錯電話號碼了。

- I'm afraid you've got the wrong number.
  你恐怕撥錯電話了。

- What number are you dialing?
  你打幾號？

- What number are you trying to reach?
  你打幾號？

- Who are you trying to reach?
  你要找哪位？

- There is no one here by that name.
  這裡沒有這個人。

會話實例

例 May I speak to Mr. Chang?
我能和張先生講話嗎？

例 Who are you trying to reach?
你要找哪位？

例 Mr. Chang.
張先生。

例 There is no one here by that name.
這裡沒有這個人。

🎧track 05-07

 公用電話

▶句型**A**◀

- Is there a pay phone here?
  這裡有公用電話嗎？

- Do you sell calling cards?
  你們有賣電話卡嗎？

- Do you sell international phone cards?
  你們有賣國際電話卡嗎？

- I need a phone card.
  我要買張電話卡。

- I need change for the pay phone.
  我需要零錢打公用電話。

- Where can I buy a phone card?
  哪裡可以買電話卡？

- I need to use a phone book.
  我需要用電話簿。

- Do you have a local phone book?
  你有本地的電話簿嗎？

會話實例

例 Is there a pay phone here?
這裡有公用電話嗎？

例 Sure, it's over there.
當然，在那兒。

▶**句型 B**◀

- We have one good for sixty minutes.
  我們有一種可以用六十分鐘的。

- You can add value.
  你可以加值。

- We do sell international phone cards.
  我們有賣國際電話卡。

會話實例

例 I need a phone card.
我要買張電話卡。

例 We have one good for sixty minutes.
我們有一種可以用六十分鐘的。

例 How much is it?
多少錢？

例 Ten dollars.
十元。

 track 05-08

Unit 8 付費電話

▶句型A◀

- Operator. May I help you?
  接線生，我可以為你服務嗎？

- Which city and number please?
  請問哪個城市及電話號碼？

- Directory assistance.
  查號台。

會話實例

例 Operator. May I help you?
接線生，我可以為你服務嗎？

- I'd like to place a collect call.
  我想打對方付費電話。

⑤ 郵寄及電話用語

- Which city and number please?
  請問哪個城市及電話號碼？
- New York, the number is 864-4727.
  紐約，電話是 864-4727。
- Who should I say is calling please?
  我要説是誰打的電話呢？
- Mary.
  瑪莉。
- OK, please stand by.
  好的，請稍等。

►句型 B◄

- I'd like to place a collect call.
  我想打對方付費電話。
- I'd like the telephone number for HP Company.
  我要查惠普公司的電話。

會話實例

例 Directory assistance.
  查號台。
例 I'd like the telephone number for Camper Company.
  我要查康普公司的電話。

例 Is that in the city, sir?
請問它在市內嗎，先生？

例 Yes, it is.
是的。

例 OK, one moment, please.
好的，請稍等。

🎧 track 05-09

Unit 9
旅館、長途電話

▶ 句型 A ◀

● I'd like to make a local call.
我想打市內電話。

● How do I call my country on my hotel room?
我要如何用旅館電話打回我國家呢？

● How do I dial out?
我要如何撥出呢？

● How much do you charge for a local call?
市內電話怎麼收費呢？

● How do you dial long distance?
怎麼打長途電話呢？

會話實例

例 Hello. How do I call my country on my hotel room?

哈囉，我要如何用旅館電話打回我國家呢？

例 First dial 19 for an open line, then dial the country code number of the country you want to call and then the number you want to call.

先撥外線碼 19，再撥你要通話國家的國碼，然後是你要打的號碼。

例 I see. Thank you.

知道了，謝謝。

▶句型 B◀

- You can look at the area code map of a phone book.

  你可以查電話簿的區域號碼地圖。

- You can call Directory assistance.

  你可以打電話問查號台。

會話實例

例 How do you dial long distance?

怎麼打長途電話呢？

例 Just dial 1, then the area code, then the number of the person you want to talk to.

撥 1，再撥區域號碼，然後是你要通話的人的號碼。

例 How do I find out the area code?

我怎麼查區域號碼呢？

例 You can look at the area code map of a phone book.

你可以查電話簿的區域號碼地圖。

例 I got it. Thanks.

我知道了，謝謝。

🎧 track 05-10

Unit 10

郵寄

▶ 句型 A ◀

- Where can I buy stamps?

  我可以在哪裡買郵票呢？

- Where is the mailbox?

  郵筒在哪兒呢？

- I'd like to mail these postcards to Taiwan.

  我想寄這些明信片到台灣。

- I need this sent overseas.

  我要把這個寄到國外。

- When will they arrive?

  什麼時候會到呢？

- How much is the postage?

  郵資是多少呢？

- What is the quickest kind of mail?

  最快的是哪一種郵寄方式？

會話實例

例 I'd like to mail these postcards to Taiwan.

  我想寄這些明信片到台灣。

例 How many stamps do you need?

  你要幾張郵票？

▶句型 B◀

- There is a stamp machine over there.

  那裡有一台郵票販售機。

- The top one is for town letters, the bottom one for out of town.
  上方那個是市內郵件的，底下那個是市外的。

- How many stamps do you need?
  你要幾張郵票？

- The postage will cost $6.75.
  郵資是 6.75 元。

會話實例

例 I need this sent overseas.
我要把這個寄到國外。

例 where to?
寄到哪裡呢？

例 Taiwan.
台灣。

例 The postage will cost $6.75.
郵資是 6.75 元。

 🎧 track 05-11

你一定要會說的10句話

1. Speaking.
   我就是，請說。

2. May I speak to John?
   我能跟約翰講電話嗎？

3. Is Amy there?
   艾咪在嗎？

4. Can I call again in 10 minutes?
   我可以十分鐘後再打過來嗎？

5. May I leave a message?
   我可以留言嗎？

6. Please tell her I called.
   請轉告她我有打電話來。

7. Is there a pay phone here?
   這裡有公用電話嗎？

8. Do you sell calling cards?
   你們有賣電話卡嗎？

9. I'd like to place a collect call.
   我想打對方付費電話。

10. How do I call my country on my hotel room?
    我要如何用旅館電話打回我國家呢？

你一定要聽懂的10句話

1. Who is calling, please?
   你是哪一位？

2. Hold on, please.
   請等一下。

3. Sorry to have kept you waiting.
   不好意思讓你等那麼久。

4. He's still on the phone.
   他還在講電話。

5. I'll put you through.
   我幫你轉接。

6. Would you like to leave a message?
   你要留言嗎？

7. There is no one here by that name.
   這裡沒有這個人。

8. You must have the wrong number.
   你一定撥錯電話號碼了。

9. Operator. May I help you?
   接線生，我可以為你服務嗎？

10. You can call Directory assistance.
    你可以打電話問查號台。

Chapter

6

住宿

Unit 1
預約住宿

▶句型A◀

- I'd like to book a room for next weekend.

  我想要預定下週末的住宿。

- Do you have any rooms available?

  請問你們還有空房嗎？

- Do you still have vacancy for two?

  你們還有兩人房的空房嗎？

- I'll book a double room.

  我要訂一間雙人房。

- For tonight only.

  只住今晚。

會話實例

例 I'd like to book a room for next weekend.

我想要預定下週末的住宿。

例 For how many people?

幾個人要住的呢？

例 Two.

兩個。

例 Eight dollars plus tax.

八元稅外加。

▶句型 B◀

- For how many people?

  幾個人要住的呢？

- Do you need a double or twin bed room?

  要雙人床還是兩個單人床的房間呢？

- How long will you be staying?

  你們要住多久？

- We recommend that you make a reservation.

  我們建議你先預約。

會話實例

例 Do you have any rooms available?

請問你們還有空房嗎？

例 For how many people?

幾個人要住的呢？

例 Four.

四個。

例 How long will you be staying?
你們要住多久？

- From this Thursday to Saturday.
  從這禮拜四到禮拜六。

- We have a few vacancies left.
  我們還有一些空房。

 🎧 track 06-02

房間種類

▶句型 A◀

- I'd like to know what types of rooms you offer.
  我想了解你們有什麼樣式的房間。

- Do you have any rooms with two double beds?
  你們有兩張雙人床的房間嗎？

- Do you have a twin-bedded room?
  你們有兩張單人床的房間嗎？

- Do you have a single room?
  你們有單人房嗎？

● Do your rooms have views?
你們房間有景觀嗎？

● Can we have a non-smoking room?
我們要禁菸的房間可以嗎？

會話實例

例 Do you have any rooms with two double beds?
你們有兩張雙人床的房間嗎？

例 Yes, we do.
是的，我們有。

例 I'll take it.
我要訂。

▶ 句型 B ◀

● We charge an extra ten dollars.
我們要加收十元。

● We have all types of accommodations available.
我們所有樣式都有。

● We have regular, deluxe and superior rooms.
我們有標準房、豪華房和高級房。

1
7

6
住
宿

- We have business rooms.
  我們有商務房。

- We have villas.
  我們有別墅。

會話實例

例 Do your rooms have views?
你們房間有景觀嗎？

例 We have lovely harbor side rooms, and park view rooms, too.
我們有美麗的面海港房間，也有面公園景色的房間。

 ∩track 06-03

房間價錢

►句型A◄

- How much is the rate?
  請問要多少錢？

- How much per night?
  請問住一晚要多少錢？

- How much would it be?
  要多少錢？

- What's today's rate for a double room?
  今天的雙人房要多少錢？

- Do you have any cheaper rooms?
  你們有便宜一點的房間嗎？

- Does it include tax?
  有含稅嗎？

- Are there any meals included?
  有包括餐點嗎？

會話實例

例 How much per night?
請問住一晚要多少錢？

例 500 dollars per night, plus tax.
含稅一晚要五百元。

▶句型B◀

- The rate for the weekend is 120 dollars a night.
  週末一晚的費用是一百二十元。

- It includes breakfast.
  有包含早餐。

會話實例

例 How much would it be?
要多少錢？

例 The rate for the weekend is 120 dollars a night.
週末一晚的費用是一百二十元。

例 Are there any meals included?
有包括餐點嗎？

例 It includes breakfast.
有包含早餐。

🎧 track 06-04

Unit 4

住宿天數

▸**句型A**◂

- I plan to stay for two nights.
  我計畫要在這裡住兩晚。

- I'm going to stay for three nights.
  我要住三晚。

- Do you have a single room for 2 nights?
  你們有單人房可以住兩晚嗎？

- Do you have a double room from Monday to Friday?
  你們還有星期一到星期五的雙人房？

會話實例

例 Do you have a double room from Monday to Friday?
你們還有星期一到星期五的雙人房嗎？

例 Let me check. Yes.
我查一下，有的。

例 OK, I'll take it.
好，我要訂。

▶句型 B◀

- How many nights will you stay?
  你想要住幾晚？

- We're all booked up.
  我們全都客滿了。

- I'm afraid we are booked that weekend.
  那個星期恐怕都已經客滿了！

- There are only a few vacancies left.
  只有剩下一些空房。

會話實例

例 May I help you?
需要我幫忙嗎?

例 Can I reserve a double room for next week?
我可以預約下星期的雙人房嗎?

例 How many nights will you stay?
你想要住幾晚?

例 3 nights. From next Monday to next Wednesday.
三個晚上,從下禮拜一到下禮拜三。

🎧 track 06-05

Unit 5
登記住宿

▶句型A◀

- What time can I check in?
  我幾點可以登記住宿?

- What time do I need to check out?
  我幾點要結帳離開飯店?

- I'd like to check in.
  我要登記住宿。

- I have a reservation for 4 nights.
  我訂了四晚的住宿。

- I didn't make a reservation.
  我沒有預約住宿。

- Here's the confirmation slip.
  這是我的確認單。

會話實例

例 May I help you, sir?
先生,需要我幫忙嗎?

例 I'd like to check in.
我要登記住宿。

例 OK, sir, may I have your name?
好的,先生,請問您的大名?

例 My name is Steven Jones.
我的名字是史蒂文瓊斯。

▶句型 B◀

- May I have your name?
  請問您的大名?

- Do you have a reservation?
  你有預約住宿嗎?

- Did you make a reservation?
  你有預約住宿嗎?

- Here's your key.
  這是你的鑰匙。

- Here's your key card.
  這是你的鑰匙卡片。

例 I want to check in.
我要登記住宿。

例 Do you have a reservation?
你有訂位嗎？

例 Yes, my name is Kelly Yang.
有，我的名字是楊凱莉。

例 Here's your key card.
這是你的鑰匙卡片。

 ∩track 06-06

Unit 6
旅館用餐

▶句型A◀

- This is your breakfast coupon.
  這是你的早餐券。

- Breakfast is served from 7 am to 10 am.
  早餐從七點到十點。

會話實例

例 This is your breakfast coupon.
這是你的早餐券。

例 When is breakfast served?
早餐幾點供應呢？

例 It's from 7 am until 10 am.
從早上七點到十點。

▶句型 B◀

- When is breakfast served?
  早餐幾點供應呢？

- Where is the breakfast room?
  早餐室在哪？

- When does your bar open?
  你們的吧台幾點開？

- I lost my breakfast coupon.
  我的早餐券不見了。

- I forgot to bring my breakfast coupons with me.
  我忘了帶早餐券。

會話書例

例 I forgot to bring my breakfast coupons with me.

我忘了帶早餐券。

例 It doesn't matter. Just tell me your room number.

沒關係，跟我說你的房間號碼就好。

track 06-07

Unit 7

飯店設施

► 句型A ◄

- When is the swimming poor open?

  請問游泳池幾點開呢？

- Will your outdoor pool be open next week?

  下星期你們的戶外游泳池會開嗎？

- I'm looking for a laundromat.

  我在找自助洗衣店。

- Do you have the laundry service?

  你們有洗衣服務嗎？

- Does your hotel have wireless Internet service?

  你們飯店有無線網路服務嗎？

- Is it free?

  是免費的嗎？

會話實例

例 Will your outdoor pool be open next week?

下星期你們的戶外游泳池會開嗎？

例 Yes.

有的。

例 Is it free?

是免費的嗎？

例 For guests it is.

住客免費。

▶句型B◀

- Our indoor pool is open.

  我們的室內游泳池有開放。

- It opens at 7am.

  早上七點開。

- We have laundry service.

  我們有洗衣服務。

會話實例

例 I'm looking for a Laundromat.
我在找自助洗衣店。

例 There's one about three blocks down on the left side of the street.
街道左邊大約三個街區左右有一間。

例 Thank you.
謝謝。

 track 06-08

客房服務

▶ 句型A ◀

● Room service. May I help you?
客房服務，有什麼需我為你服務的？

● Your room number, please.
請問你的房號。

● Do you need anything else?
還有其他需要嗎？

會話實例

例 Room service. May I help you?
客房服務，有什麼需要我服務的？

例 I'd like an extra pillow for room 617.
我要在617號房多加一個枕頭。

例 No problem, sir. Do you need anything else?
沒問題，先生，還有其他需要嗎？

▶句型B◀

- I'd like to order room service, please.
  我要客房送餐服務。

- I'd like to order some coffee and toast.
  我要點一些咖啡和土司。

- Will you send up two cups of coffee, please?
  請你送兩杯咖啡上來，謝謝！

- We need an extra towel.
  我們需要多一條毛巾。

- We need more toilet paper.
  我們需要多一些衛生紙。

- I need a hair dryer.
  我需要吹風機。

- I need a power converter.
  我需要一個電源轉換器。

- I need a plug-in adapter for my laptop.
  我的筆記型電腦需要一個轉接頭。

會話實例

例 Room service. May I help you?
  客房服務，有什麼需要我服務的？

例 We need an extra towel.
  我們需要多一條毛巾。

track 06-09

Unit
9
飯店設施出問題

▶句型A◀

- Reception desk. May I help you?
  接待櫃台。我可以幫你嗎？

- I'll send someone immediately to check
  for you.
  我會馬上派人去幫你檢查。

會話實例

例 Reception desk. May I help you?
接待櫃台。我可以幫你嗎？

例 The lamp in my room doesn't work.
我房裡的燈壞了。

例 Sorry, madam. I'll have someone from housekeeping go fix it immediately.
抱歉，女士，我會立刻叫服務人員去處理。

例 Thank you.
謝謝。

▶句型 B◀

- My phone is out of order.
  我的電話故障了。

- The air conditioner makes a funny noise.
  空調有奇怪的聲音。

- There is no hot water in my room.
  我房間沒有熱水。

- The dryer doesn't work.
  吹風機壞了。

- The toilet doesn't flush.
  馬桶不能沖水。

- The bulb burnt out.
  燈泡燒壞了。

會話實例

例 Reception desk. May I help you?
接待櫃台。我可以幫你嗎？

例 There is no hot water in my room.
我房間沒有熱水。

例 I'll send someone immediately to check for you.
我會馬上派人去幫你檢查。

例 Thank you.
謝謝。

 ∩ track 06-10

Unit 10
換房

▶句型 A◀

- I'd like to change my room.
  我想換房間。

- I'd like to have a different room.
  我想換房間。

- Do you have a larger room available?
  你們有大一點的房間嗎？

- I'd like to have a better room.
  我想要一間比較好的房間。

會話實例

例 How may I help you?
需要我幫忙嗎？

例 I'd like to change my room.
我想換房間。

▶句型B◀

- How may I help you?
  需要我幫忙嗎？

- Is there a problem?
  有什麼問題嗎？

會話實例

例 I'd like to have a different room.
我想換房間。

例 Is there a problem, sir?
有什麼問題嗎，先生？

例 Yes. Mine faces the street. It's too noisy.
我的房間面對街道太吵了。

- I understand. I'll find a quieter one for you.
  我瞭解了，我會找間安靜點的給你。

🎧 track 06-11

你一定要會說的10句話

1. Do you have any rooms available?
   請問你們還有空房嗎？
2. Do you have any rooms with two double beds?
   你們有兩張雙人床的房間嗎？
3. How much per night?
   請問住一晚要多少錢？
4. Are there any meals included?
   有包括餐點嗎？
5. I plan to stay for two nights.
   我計畫要在這裡住兩晚。
6. What time do I need to check out?
   我幾點要結帳離開飯店？
7. When is breakfast served?
   早餐幾點供應呢？
8. Does your hotel have wireless Internet service?
   你們飯店有無線網路服務嗎？

6
住宿

9. The dryer doesn't work.
吹風機壞了。

10. I'd like to change my room.
我想換房間。

你一定要聽懂的10句話

1. How long will you be staying?
你們要住多久？

2. We charge an extra ten dollars.
我們要加收十元。

3. How many nights will you stay?
你想要住幾晚？

4. We're all booked up.
我們全都客滿了。

5. May I have your name?
請問您的大名？

6. Do you have a reservation?
你有預約住宿嗎？

7. We have regular, deluxe and superior rooms.
我們有標準房、豪華房和高級房。

8. It includes breakfast.
有包含早餐。

9. Room service. May I help you?
   客房服務，有什麼需要我服務的？
10. Your room number, please.
    請問你的房號。

Chapter

7

飲食

選擇餐廳

▶句型A◀

● Do you know of any good restaurants?
你知道有什麼好餐廳嗎?

● Do you serve Chinese food here?
你們有中國菜嗎?

● May I see the menu?
我可以看菜單嗎?

● I'd like to see the dessert menu.
我想看甜點單。

● Is there a smoking section here?
這裡有吸菸區嗎?

● Is there live music tonight?
今晚有現場演奏嗎?

會話實例

例 Do you know of any good restaurants?
你知道有什麼好餐廳嗎?

例 There is a good one down the street.
這條街直走有一家不錯。

例 What is its name?

叫什麼名字呢？

例 L'Appetit.

拉佩提。

▶ 句型 B ◀

● It has great Italian food.

它的義大利食物很棒。

● We have both Western and Chinese dishes.

我們有西式及中式菜餚。

會話實例

例 Do you serve Chinese food here?

你們有中國菜嗎？

例 Yes, we have both Western and Chinese dishes.

有的，我們有西式及中式菜餚。

track 07-02

餐廳訂位

►句型A◄

● I'd like to make a reservation.
我想訂位。

● Do you have any tables available for tonight?
你們今晚有任何空位嗎？

● I'd like to make a reservation for tomorrow.
我想預訂明天的位子。

會話實例

例 Hello. Danny's Restaurant.
你好，丹尼餐廳。

例 Hello. I'd like to make a reservation for tonight.
你好，我想預定今晚的位子。

例 How many will be in your party?
你們會有幾位？

例 There will be 7.
會有七位。

例 What time will you arrive?

你們幾點會到呢？

● Around seven.

大約七點。

▶句型B◀

● What time will you arrive?

你們幾點會到呢？

● We look forward to seeing you.

我們期待見到你們。

會話實例

例 I'd like to make a reservation for tonight.

我想預訂今晚的位子。

例 How many and when?

幾位和幾點呢？

例 Two people and we'll arrive at seven o'clock.

兩人，我們七點會到。

例 All right. We look forward to seeing you.

沒問題，期待見到你們。

Unit 3 事先及現場訂位

▶句型 A◀

- Did you have a reservation?
  你們有訂位嗎?

- Welcome.
  歡迎光臨。

- How many?
  幾位?

- For how many people?
  幾位?

- Smoking or non-smoking?
  吸菸還是不吸菸呢?

會話實例

例 Good evening. Two for dinner?
晚安,兩人用晚餐嗎?

例 Yes.
是的。

例 Did you have a reservation?
你們有訂位嗎?

例 Yes, I made a reservation at six.

有，我訂了六點鐘的位子。

▶ 句型 B ◀

● I made a reservation at six.
我訂了六點鐘的位子。

● We had a reservation.
我們有訂位。

● Do you have a table available?
你們現在還有位子嗎？

● A table for two.
兩位，謝謝。

● There are four of us.
我們有四個人。

會話實例

例 Welcome to Karin's Restaurant.
歡迎光臨卡琳餐廳。

例 I want a table for six, please.
我要六人的位子。

例 Wait a moment, sir.
先生，請稍等一下。

track 07-04

Unit 4 餐廳客滿

▶句型A◀

- Do you have a table available?
  請問還有空位嗎？

- How long do we have to wait?
  我們要等多久？

- We can wait.
  我們可以等。

- It's too late!
  太晚了！

會話實例

例 Do you have a table available?
請問還有空位嗎？

例 I'm sorry. We are quite full tonight
很抱歉，今晚都客滿了。

例 How long do we have to wait?
我們要等多久？

例 I'm afraid you have to wait for one hour. Is it OK?
大概要等一小時，可以嗎？

例 It's too late!

太晚了！

▶ 句型 B ◀

- We are quite full tonight.

  今晚都客滿了。

- It's bookcd up tonight.

  今晚沒有空位了。

- I'm afraid all our tables are taken.

  恐怕我們所有的位子都坐滿了。

- There are no tables now.

  現在沒有座位。

- Would you mind waiting for thirty minutes?

  你介不介意等三十分鐘呢？

會話實例

例 How long do we have to wait?

我們要等多久？

例 Would you mind waiting for thirty minutes?

你介不介意等三十分鐘呢？

例 That all right. We can wait.

沒關係，我們可以等。

Unit 5 帶位

②④⑤

⑦ 飲食

► 句型 A ◄

● We have a table for you now.
我們現在有座位給你了。

● This way, please.
這邊請。

● I'm sorry to have kept you waiting.
抱歉讓你久等了。

● We're very sorry for the delay.
非常抱歉耽擱您的時間。

● How about this table?
這個座位如何？

● Would you like a window seat?
你們要靠窗的座位嗎？

● The view here is great.
這裡的景觀很漂亮。

● Is this fine with you?
這個座位好嗎？

會話實例

例 This way, please.
這邊請。

例 We'd like the seat near the window.
我們想要靠窗的位子。

▶句型 B ◀

- I don't like this area.
  我不喜歡這一區。

- Not close to the gate.
  不要離門口太近。

- I'd like the seat far away from the restroom.
  我想要離廁所遠一點的位子。

- We'd like the seat near the window.
  我們想要靠窗的位子。

- We'd like the table by the window.
  我們想要靠窗的位子。

- We'd like the seat at the corner.
  我們想要靠角落的位子。

- Can we have a quieter table?
  我們可以選安靜一點的座位嗎？

會話實例

例 How about this table?
這個座位如何？

例 I don't like this area. May we have those two seats?
我不喜歡這一區，我們可以坐那兩個座位嗎？

例 Sure. Please be seated.
當然，請坐。

 ⌂track 07-06

Unit 6

詢問點餐

▶句型A◀

● May I take your order now?
現在要點餐了嗎？

● Are you ready to order?
準備好點餐了嗎？

● I'll be right back for your order.
我馬上回來為您點餐。

● I'll be right back with you.
我待會回來。

- Take your time.
  慢慢來。

會話實例

例 May I take your order now?
現在要點餐了嗎？

例 Yes, I'd like a chicken sandwich.
我要雞肉三明治。

例 How about you, sir?
好的，先生，你要什麼呢？

例 I'll order the same thing.
我也要點一樣的。

▶句型 B◀

- May I see the menu, please?
  請給我看菜單。

- Can we order later?
  我們可以等一下再點餐嗎？

- We're not ready to order.
  我們還沒準備好要點餐。

- I haven't decided yet.
  我還沒有決定好。

- Could you give us a few minutes?
  可以給我們幾分鐘看菜單嗎？

- We'll let you know if we are ready to order.

  我們準備好要點餐再跟你說。

會話實例

例 Are you ready to order?

準備好點餐了嗎？

例 We're not ready to order.

我們還沒準備好要點餐。

例 Sure, please take your time.

好的，請慢慢看。

🎧 track 07-07

Unit 7

今日特餐、招牌菜

▶句型 A◀

- Are you ready to order?

  你們準備好要點餐了嗎？

- You should try our seafood.

  你應該要試試我們的海鮮。

- Rabbit with Mustard Sauce is the specialty of the house.

  兔肉佐芥末是本店招牌菜。

會話實例

例 Are you ready to order?
你們準備好要點餐了嗎？

例 What is today's special?
今日特餐是什麼呢？

例 Chicken fajitas.
雞肉口袋餅。

例 What else is included?
還有包含什麼呢？

例 The meal includes soup and salad.
包含湯和沙拉。

▶句型B◀

● What is today's special?
今日特餐是什麼呢？

● What's the specialty of the restaurant?
餐廳的招牌菜是什麼？

● What's popular here?
這裡什麼受歡迎呢？

● What's the house special?
本店特餐是什麼呢？

● Do you have a set meal for two?
你們有兩人套餐嗎？

● What do you recommend we to try?
你建議我們試什麼呢？

會話實例

例 What's the specialty of the restaurant?
餐廳的招牌菜是什麼？

例 It's Rib's Eye Steak.
是肋眼牛排。

例 OK. I'd like to order Rib Eye Steak.
好的，我點肋眼牛排。

🎧track 07-08

沙拉、主菜

►**句型A**◄

● What do you want for salad?
你要什麼沙拉呢？

● What kind of salad dressing would you prefer?
請問你要哪一種沙拉佐料？

● Would you like an appetizer?
你要開胃菜嗎？

2
5
1

7
飲
食

- How do you want it cooked?
  你要幾分熟？

- Do you want steak sauce?
  你要牛排醬嗎？

會話實例

例 What do you want for salad?
你要什麼沙拉呢？

例 I'd like the Caeser Salad.
我要點凱薩沙拉。

▶句型 B◀

- What salad do you have?
  你們有什麼沙拉？

- I'd like to order steak.
  我要點牛排。

- May I see the drink list?
  我可以看一下飲料單嗎？

- I'll have salmon.
  我要點鮭魚。

- I'd like my steak medium, please.
  我想要我的牛排五分熟。

- Rare, please.
  三分熟。

- Mcdium, please.
  五分熟。

- Well-done, please.
  全熟。

例 How do you want it cooked?
你要幾分熟？

例 Medium rare, please.
五分熟。

 ⌂track 07-09

(Unit 9)

湯點、甜點、飲料

▶句型A◀

- What would you like for the soup?
  你要喝什麼湯？

- How about the dessert?
  甜點要點什麼呢？

- Which flavor would you prefer?
  你要什麼口味？

- Anything to drink?
  要喝點什麼嗎？

- Would you like something to drink?
  需要點飲料嗎？

- Which would you prefer, coffee or tea?
  你要點咖啡還是茶？

- Here are your drinks.
  這是您的飲料。

- When would you like your coffee?
  你要什麼時候上咖啡？

會話實例

例 What would you like for the soup?
你要喝什麼湯？

例 I want to try seafood soup.
我要點海鮮湯。

▶句型B◀

- I want to try pumpkin soup.
  我想試一試南瓜湯。

- May I see your drink list?
  可以看你們的飲料單嗎？

- Do you have beer?
  你們有啤酒嗎？

- Coffee would be fine.
  我點咖啡。

- We want our drinks with our dinner.
  我們想邊喝飲料邊用餐。

- We'll have drinks later.
  我們要晚點喝飲料。

- What kind of pie do you have?
  你們有什麼口味的派？

- I want to have a brownie.
  我要點布朗尼蛋糕。

會話實例

例 May I see your drink list?
可以看你們的飲料單嗎？

例 OK. I'll get one for you.
好的，我拿一份給你。

 ∩track 07-10

完成點餐

▶句型A◀

- Is that all for your order?
  你點的就這些嗎？

- What else are you going to have?
  你還要點什麼嗎？

● Is there anything else?
還要不要別的？

● Anything else?
還有沒有要其他餐點呢？

● Will that be all?
就這樣？

會話實例

例 Is that all for your order?
你點的就這些嗎？

例 That's all for us.
我們就點這些。

▶句型 B◀

● That's all for us.
我們就點這些。

● I think it's enough now.
我想這就夠了。

● Can we order that later?
我們可以等一下再點嗎？

會話實例

例 Would you like something to drink?
需要點飲料嗎？

例 Can we order that later?
我們可以等一下再點嗎？

例 Of course.
當然可以。

track 07-11

Unit 11 要求服務

▶句型A◀

● Would you bring us some bread?
能給我一些麵包嗎？

● Can I have more water, please?
能多給我一點水嗎？

● More dipping sauce, please.
請多點沾醬。

● More chips, please.
請多給點脆片。

● I need a straw, please.
我需要一根吸管。

● Do you have chopsticks?
你們有筷子嗎？

● May I have a refill?
我可以續杯嗎？

會話實例

例 Excuse me.
不好意思。

例 May I help you?
需要我幫忙嗎？

例 Would you bring us some bread?
能給我一些麵包嗎？

例 Yes, I'll be right back.
好的，我馬上回來。

▶ **句型B** ◀

● Of course.
當然。

● I'll be right back.
我馬上回來。

● May I help you?
需要我幫忙嗎？

會話實例

例 Can I have more water, please?
能多給我一點水嗎？

- Yes, of course.
  當然。

track 07-12

Unit 12 送餐、送錯餐點

▶句型A◀

- May I serve your meal now?
  現在可以上你的餐點嗎？

- Who has the New York Steak?
  誰點紐約牛排？

- May I serve your soup now?
  我現在可以上您的湯點嗎？

- Please have them with this saucc.
  請沾這個醬料食用。

- Is this yours?
  這是你的嗎？

- What was your order?
  你點什麼？

- I'll check your order right now.
  我馬上查你的餐點。

● I'm very sorry for the mistake.

很抱歉弄錯了。

會話實例

例 May I serve your meal now?

現在可以上你的餐點嗎？

例 Yes, please.

好的，請。

▶句型B◀

● That's not what I ordered.

那不是我點的。

● Is there a dish missing?

是不是少上一道菜？

● I'm afraid there is a dish missing.

恐怕有道餐點沒來。

會話實例

例 You ordered the stcak, right?

你點牛排嗎？

例 No, that's not what I ordered.

不是，那不是我點的。

例 What was your order?

你點什麼？

例 I ordered Roast Chicken.
我點烤雞。

● I'm very sorry for the mistake.
很抱歉弄錯了。

 track 07-13

打翻東西

►句型A◄

● I spilled my drink.
我打翻飲料了。

● Could you bring us a few napkins?
你可以給我們一些紙巾嗎？

● I dropped my spoon on the floor.
我的叉子掉到地上了。

● The fork is a little dirty.
這隻叉子有點髒。

● This glass is cracked.
這個玻璃杯有裂痕。

● My plate is chipped.
我的盤子有缺口。

● May I have a new one?

可以再給我一隻新的嗎？

會話實例

例 I spilled my drink.

我打翻飲料了。

例 I'll clean it up for you.

我幫您整理。

例 Thank you.

謝謝。

▶句型 B◀

● I'll change a new one for you.

我幫你換一支新的。

● I'll bring you a few napkins.

我給我們一些紙巾。

● I'll clean it up for you.

我幫您整理。

會話實例

例 Waiter!

服務生！

例 Yes, sir?

先生，有什麼事？

例 The fork is a little dirty. May I have a new one?

這隻叉子有點髒。可以再給我一隻新的嗎？

例 OK. I'll change a new one for you.

好的，我幫你換一支新的。

Unit
14

track 07-14

整理桌子

▶句型 A◀

● Are you finished or still working on it?
請問您用完餐還是要繼續用餐？

● May I clear your table?
我可以為您清理桌子嗎？

● Are you enjoying your meal?
您喜歡您的餐點嗎？

● May I take your plate now?
我可以收走您的盤子嗎？

會話實例

例 Are you finished or still working on it?
請問您用完餐還是要繼續用餐？

例 We have finished it.

我們吃完了。

例 May I clear your table?

我可以為您清理桌子嗎？

例 Please.

麻煩你。

▶句型 B◀

● We have finished it.

我們吃完了。

● I'm still working on it.

我還在用餐。

● Please leave that.

那個請留下來。

● Would you clear the table for us?

你可以為我們整理一下桌子嗎？

● Would you take this, please?

可以請你把這個收走嗎？

● We'd like to take the leftover food home.

我們要將剩餘的食物帶回家。

● Please box these up.

請把這些用盒子裝起來。

會話實例

例 Would you clear the table for us?

你可以為我們整理一下桌子嗎？

例 Sure.

好的。

 ∩ track 07-15

Unit 15

買單

►**句型 A**◄

● Bill, please.

請買單。

● Our bill, please.

我們的帳單，麻煩你。

● Check, please.

請結帳。

● Can I have the check, please?

請結帳。

● I'll pay it by credit card.

我要用信用卡結帳。

● I'll pay it by cash.

我要用現金付錢。

● Is the service charge included?

有包含服務費嗎？

● Is there a service charge here?

這裡有收服務費嗎？

會話實例

例 Is the service charge included?

有包含服務費嗎？

例 Yes. The 10% service charge is included.

有的，包含百分之十的服務費。

▶ 句型 B ◀

● Cash or credit card?

用現金還是用信用卡付帳？

● Would you pay it by cash or credit card?

你要用現金還是信用卡付帳？

會話實例

例 Bill, please.

請買單。

例 Cash or credit card?

用現金還是用信用卡付帳？

例 Do you accept Visa?

你們有收 Visa 卡嗎？

 track 07-16

例 Yes, we do.

　　有的。

Unit 16 速食店點餐

▶句型A◀

- I'd like a Bacon Chccscburger.

　　我要一個培根起司漢堡。

- To go, please.

　　外帶，謝謝。

- I'll have a piece of apple pie.

　　我要一個蘋果派。

會話實例

例 I'd like a Bacon Cheeseburger.

　　我要一個培根起司漢堡。

例 For here or to go?

　　要內用還外帶？

例 To go, please.

　　外帶，謝謝。

例 How about something to drink?

　　要喝點什麼嗎？

例 A coke, please.
一杯可樂，謝謝。

例 OK. Wait a moment, please.
好的，請等一下。

▶ 句型 B ◀

- For here or to go?
  要內用還外帶？

- Will that be for here or to go?
  請問你要內用還外帶？

- What can I get for you?
  你要點什麼呢？

- How about something to drink?
  要喝點什麼嗎？

- Anything else?
  還需要什麼嗎？

- Wait a moment, please.
  請等一下。

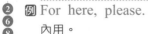
會話實例

例 Will that be for here or to go?
請問你要內用還外帶？

例 For here, please.
內用。

例 Anything else?

還需要什麼嗎？

例 I think it's enough.

我想這就夠了。

 🎧 track 07-17

你一定要聽懂的10句話

1. Did you have a reservation?

   你們有訂位嗎？

2. Smoking or non-smoking?

   吸菸還是不吸菸呢？

3. We are quite full tonight.

   今晚都客滿了。

4. Would you mind waiting for thirty minutes?

   你介不介意等三十分鐘呢？

5. We have a table for you now.

   我們現在有座位給你了。

6. May I take your order now?

   現在要點餐了嗎？

7. Which flavor would you prefer?

   你要什麼口味？

8. May I clear your table?
   我可以為您清理桌子嗎？
9. Cash or credit card?
   用現金還是用信用卡付帳？
10. For here or to go?
    要內用還外帶？

你一定要會說的 10 句話

1. I'd like to make a reservation.
   我想訂位。
2. May I see the menu?
   我可以看菜單嗎？
3. Do you have a table available?
   你們現在還有位子嗎？
4. We'd like the seat near the window.
   我們想要靠窗的位子。
5. We're not ready to order.
   我們還沒準備好要點餐。
6. What is today's special?
   今日特餐是什麼呢？

2
7
1

7 飲食

7. I'd like my steak medium, please.
   我想要我的牛排五分熟。

8. I'd like to order steak.
   我要點牛排。

9. Would you clear the table for us?
   你可以為我們整理一下桌子嗎？

10. Bill, please.
    請買單。

Chapter

購物

track 08-01

Unit 1
尋找物品

▶句型A◀

- Where is the produce department?
  哪裡是農產品區呢？

- Do you have a deli here?
  你們有熟食區嗎？

- In which section can I find the soap?
  肥皂在哪一區？

- How should I get to the shoe department?
  鞋區在哪裡？

會話實例

例 Where is the produce department?
哪裡是農產品區呢？

例 It's on Aisle 5.
在五號走道。

▶句型B◀

- It's on Aisle 5.
  在五號走道。

- It's on the 2nd floor.
  在二樓。

會話實例

例 How should I get to the shoe department?

鞋區在哪裡？

例 It's on the 2nd floor.

在二樓。

🎧 track 08-02

Unit 2

只看不買

►句型A◄

- May I help you?
  需要我的幫忙嗎？

- Do you need some help?
  需要幫忙嗎？

會話實例

例 May I help you?

需要我的幫忙嗎？

274

例 I'm just looking around.
我只是隨便看看。

▶ 句型 B ◀

● I'm just looking around.
我只是隨便看看。

● No, thanks.
不用,謝謝!

● I don't need any help.
我不需要任何服務。

● Not yet. Thanks.
還不需要,謝謝!

● Maybe later. Thank you.
也許等一下要,謝謝!

會話實例

例 May I help you with something?
需要我的幫忙嗎?

例 No, thanks.
不用,謝謝!

尋找特定商品

▶句型 A◀

- What are you looking for?
  你在找什麼嗎？

- Is there anything special in mind?
  心裡有想好要什麼嗎？

- Is it a present for someone?
  送給誰的禮物嗎？

- What do you want to buy?
  你想買什麼？

- Have a look.
  請看看！

會話實例

例 What are you looking for?
你在找什麼嗎？

例 I'd like a scarf for my dress.
我想要一條圍巾搭配我的洋裝。

例 OK, would you like to take a look at this?
好的，你要看一下這個嗎？

▶句型B◀

● I'd like a scarf for my dress.
我想要一條圍巾搭配我的洋裝。

● I'm looking for a light bulb for this lamp.
我在找適用這個燈的電燈泡。

● I'm looking for baseball hats.
我在找棒球帽。

● I need to buy a birthday present for my son.
我要幫兒子買生日禮物。

● I'm looking for some Christmas presents for my kids.
我在找一些要送給孩子們的禮物。

● I'm trying to find a sweater for my son.
我想幫兒子買毛衣。

會話實例

例 What do you want to buy?
你想買什麼？

例 I need to buy a birthday present for my son.
我要幫兒子買生日禮物。

例 Is there anything special in mind?
心裡有想好要什麼嗎？

例 I'm not sure. Maybe you can help me.
我也不是很確定，也許你可以幫我。

Unit
4

🎧 track 08-04

參觀商品

►句型A◄

● May I see those pair of shoes?
我可以看看那雙鞋嗎？

● I'd like to see some sport watches.
我想看一些運動錶。

● Please show me that black sweater.
請給我看看那件黑色毛衣。

● May I have a look at them?
我可以看看它們嗎？

● Show me that hat.
給我看那個帽子。

會話實例

2
7
8

例 May I help you?
需要我的幫忙嗎？

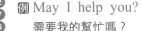

例 Those pants look great. May I have a look at them?

那些褲子看起來不錯，我可以看看它們嗎？

例 Sure. Here you are.

好的，給你。

▶ 句型 B ◀

● What would you like to see?

你想看些什麼？

● Which one do you like?

你喜歡哪一個？

● Please have a look.

請看看！

● Here you are.

給你。

會話實例

例 What would you like to see?

你想看些什麼？

例 I'd like to see some belts.

我想看一些皮帶。

例 Please have a look.

請看看！

🎧 track 08-05

Unit 5

評論商品

▶句型 A◀

- Did you find something you like?

  有找到喜歡的東西了嗎?
- Is that what you are looking for?

  你要找的是這一種嗎?
- How about this?

  這個怎麼樣?
- You might be interested in those new arrivals.

  你可能會對這些新貨有興趣。

會話實例

例 Did you find something you like?

有找到喜歡的東西了嗎?

例 I'm interested in this one.

我對這個有興趣。

▶句型 B◀

- It looks nice.

  這個看起來不錯。

- I'm interested in this one.
  我對這個有興趣。

- I don't like this one.
  我不喜歡這個。

- I don't like this kind of style.
  我不喜歡這種款式。

- Can you show me something different?
  你可以給我看一些不一樣的嗎？

- It's not what I need.
  這不是我需要的。

- It's not what I'm looking for.
  這不是我要找的。

- Is that all?
  全部就只有這樣嗎？

8
購
物

會話實例

例 You might be interested in those new arrivals.
  你可能會對這些新貨有興趣。

例 They are not what I'm looking for.
  這些不是我在找的那種。

介紹、操作產品

▶句型A◀

● Would you show me how it works?
你可以操作給我看嗎？

● Can I pick it up?
我可以拿起來看看嗎？

● How to use this?
這要怎麼用？

● How do I operate it?
我要怎麼操作它？

會話書例

例 Would you show me how it works?
你可以操作給我看嗎？

例 Sure. You can push this button to turn it on.
好的，你可以按這個鈕來開啟電源。

▶句型B◀

● They are new arrivals.
它們都是新到的產品。

- Let me show you this one.
  來看看這個。

會話實例

例 They are new arrivals.
它們都是新到的產品。

例 Can I pick it up?
我可以拿起來看看嗎？

例 Sure.
當然。

🎧 track 08-07

Unit 7
產品保固

▶句型A◀

- Does it have a warranty?
  這個有保固期嗎？

- How long is the warranty on this cell phone?
  這支手機的保固期是多久？

- Do you offer a one-year warranty?
  你們有提供一年的保固嗎？

- Do you offer a life-time warranty?

  你們有提供終身的保固嗎？

- Do you offer an extended warranty for this?

  你們有提供延長保固嗎？

- What does the warranty cover?

  這保固保障什麼？

- Is the repair free in Taiwan with this warranty?

  有這個一年保固在台灣修理是免費嗎？

會話實例

例 Does it have a warranty?

  這個有保固期嗎？

例 Yes, it's a one-year warranty.

  有的，它有一年保固。

▶句型 B◀

- It's a one-year warranty.

  它有一年保固。

- Would you like to buy extended warranty protection?

  你要買延長保固嗎？

會話實例

例 Would you like to buy extended warranty protection?

你要買延長保固嗎？

例 What is that?

那是什麼？

例 It's a special service contract that protects you against extra charges.

是保障你不必額外付費的特別服務契約。

例 OK. I'll think about it.

好的，我考慮看看。

track 08-08

尺寸、顏色

▶句型A◀

- Any other sizes?
  有沒有其他尺寸？

- I don't know my size.
  我不知道我的尺寸。

- My size is 9.
  我的尺寸是九號。

- Give me size 8.
  給我八號。

- My size is between 7 and 8.
  我的尺寸介於七號和八號之間。

- I want the large size.
  我要大尺寸的。

- Do you have any ones in gray?
  你們有灰色的嗎？

- Do you have any other colors?
  還有其他顏色嗎？

會話實例

例 What is your size?
你穿什麼尺寸？

例 My size is 9.
我的尺寸是九號。

▶句型 B◀

- What is your size?
  你穿什麼尺寸？

- How about size 8?
  八號可以嗎？

- What color do you like?
  你要哪一個顏色？

- Which color do you prefer?

  你比較喜歡哪個顏色？

- You need a larger size.

  你需要大一點的。

例 What color do you like?

你要哪一個顏色？

例 Size 8 in black.

黑色的八號尺寸。

Unit 9

試穿

🎧 track 08-09

▶句型A◀

- Would you like to try it on?

  你要試穿看看嗎？

- You can try this on.

  你可以試穿這一件。

- The fitting room is right on your left side.

  更衣室就在你左手邊。

會話實例

例 Would you like to try it on?
你要試穿看看嗎？

例 No, thanks.
不用了，謝謝！

▶句型 B◀

- Can I try it on?
  我可以試穿嗎？
- Where is the fitting room?
  更衣室在哪裡？
- Where is the dressing room?
  更衣室在哪裡？
- Where can I try this on?
  我要在哪試穿？

會話實例

例 Can I try it on?
我可以試穿嗎？

例 Sure. This way, please.
當然，這邊請。

track 08-10

Unit 10

試穿結果

▶ 句型 **A** ◀

- How does this look on me?
  我穿這件看起來怎麼樣？

- Where is the mirror?
  鏡子在哪裡？

- Don't you think it's too loose?
  你不覺得太寬了嗎？

- Can I try a larger one?
  我可以試穿大一點的嗎？

- I should try another bigger one.
  我應該要穿另一件大一點的。

- It feels tight.
  有點緊。

- They were just too small.
  它們太小了。

- They seem a little big.
  好像有一點大。

會話實例

例 How does this look on me?

我穿這件看起來怎麼樣？

例 It looks perfect on you.

非常好看。

▶句型B◀

● It looks great on you.

很好看。

● It's great.

好看。

● Not bad.

不錯。

● I don't think this is good.

我不覺得這件好看。

● Would you like to try on a larger size?

你要試穿大一點的尺寸嗎？

● Does it fit?

合身嗎？

會話實例

例 Does it fit?

合身嗎？

例 It really feels tight.
真的有點緊。

track 08-11

缺貨

▶ 句 型 **A** ◀

- I think we're out of your size.
  你要的尺寸賣完了。

- We don't have any left.
  我們沒有貨了。

- We have your size, but not in that color.
  我們有你的尺寸但不是那個顏色。

例 Do you have black boots, size 38?
你們有尺寸三十八的黑靴子嗎？

例 I think we're out of your size. The closest we have is a 39.
你要的尺寸賣完了，我們有的最接近的是三十九號。

例 Do you think you'll be getting anymore in?

你們還會再進貨嗎？

例 Let's me ask for you.

我幫你問看看。

▶ 句型 B ◀

● Do you think you'll be getting anymore in?

你們還會再進貨嗎？

● Can you order one for me?

你可以幫我訂一件嗎？

會話實例

例 We have your size, but not in that color.

我們有你的尺寸但不是那個顏色。

例 Do you think you'll be getting anymore in?

你們還會再進貨嗎？

例 No, but we might have them at our other store.

不會，但我們其它倉庫可能有貨。

例 Can you order one for me?

你可以幫我訂一件嗎？

- Sure. Just give me your name and address.

  當然可以，請給我你的名字和地址。

Unit 12 詢問商品

track 08-12

8 購物

►句型 A◄

- Is it made of genuine leather?

  這是真皮做的嗎？

- What material is this made of?

  這是什麼材質做的？

- Will it shrink?

  會縮水嗎？

- Will the color fade?

  會褪色嗎？

- Can I put it in a dryer?

  可以烘乾嗎？

- Should this be dry cleaned?

  這必須乾洗嗎？

- Are those all washable?

  這些都可以水洗嗎？

● Is that all you have?

你們只有這些？

會話實例

例 Is it made of genuine leather?

這是真皮做的嗎？

例 Yes.

是的。

▶句型B◀

● This comes in many colors.

還有很多顏色。

● Which brand do you want?

你想要哪個牌子？

● What style would you like to see?

你想要看哪種款式？

會話實例

例 How much is this jacket?

這件外套要多少錢？

例 It costs $125.

要125元。

例 Is that all you have?

你們只有這些？

- This comes in many colors.
  還有很多顏色。

Unit 13
詢問售價、購買

▶ 句型 A ◀

- How much does it cost?
  這個多少錢？

- What's the price?
  價錢是多少

- Does this include tax?
  這個有含稅嗎？

- I'll take it.
  我要買！

- I'll buy this one.
  我要買這個。

- Let me think about it.
  讓我考慮一下。

- No, thanks.
  不了，謝謝。

- Not for this time.

  這次先不要買。

會話實例

例 Would you like to buy it?

你要買嗎？

例 No, thanks.

不了，謝謝。

▶**句型B**◀

- Would you like to buy it?

  你要買嗎？

- I'm sorry that I can't give you a discount.

  很抱歉我不能給你折扣。

- If you take two, I'll give you a better price.

  你如果買兩件，我就算你便宜些。

會話實例

例 How much does it cost?

這個多少錢？

例 It's $130.

130元。

例 Does this include tax?

這個有含稅嗎？

例 Yes, it does.

有。

例 OK. I'll take it.

好，我要買！

track 08-14

Unit 14 殺價

▶句型 A◀

- Are there any discounts?

請問有折扣嗎？

- Is it possible to get a discount?

可以打折嗎？

- Is there a discount for two?

買兩件可以有折扣吧。

- Will you give me a better price?

你可以算便宜一點嗎？

- Can you lower the price?

可以算便宜一點嗎？

- Can you lower it to two hundred?

可以便宜兩百塊嗎？

- How about three hundred dollars?
  可以算三百嗎？

- It's too expensive.
  太貴了。

會話實例

例 It's too expensive. Are there any discounts?
太貴了。請問有折扣嗎？

例 I'm afraid not.
抱歉，不行。

▶句型 B◀

- I can give you a 10% discount.
  我可以給你九折。

會話實例

例 Is there a discount for two?
買兩件可以有折扣吧。

例 I can give you a 10% discount.
我可以給你九折。

例 OK. I'll take it.
好的，我要買。

track 08-15

結帳、要求收據

8 購物

▶句型A◀

- Can I have a receipt?
  可以給我收據嗎？

- I'll pay cash.
  我要付現。

- I don't have a membership card.
  我沒有會員卡。

- Is it useful to be a member?
  當會員有用嗎？

- How do I become a member?
  我要如何成為會員？

會話實例

例 How would you like to pay?
你要怎麼付款？

例 I'll pay cash.
我要付現。

▶句型 B◀

- Do you have your membership card?
  你有會員卡嗎？

- That will be $5.78, please.
  總共是 5.78 元。

- How would you like to pay?
  你要怎麼付款？

- Will this be cash, check or credit card?
  你要付現、開支票還是刷卡呢？

- Do you need a receipt?
  你需要收據嗎？

- Here's the change.
  零錢在這裡。

會話實例

例 Do you need a receipt?
你需要收據嗎？

例 Yes, please.
要，謝謝。

track 08-16

Unit
16
包裝

▶句型A◀

● Could you wrap it up for me?
你能幫我打包嗎？

● Could you pack it for me?
你能幫我裝起來嗎？

● Would you put them in a box?
你可以把它們放進盒子裡嗎？

● Would you wrap it as a present?
你可以幫把它包裝成禮物嗎？

● I'd like this wrapped.
我要包裝這個。

● Will you wrap them up separately?
能請你分開包裝嗎？

● This needs to be carefully wrapped.
這要小心包裝。

● I need it boxed securely.
我要安全地把它裝箱。

會話實例

例 Could you wrap it up for me?
你能幫我打包嗎？

例 Sure.
好的。

▶句型 B◀

● Would you wait for a second?
能請你稍等一下嗎？

● Sorry, we don't have this service.
抱歉，我們沒有這項服務。

會話實例

例 Would you wrap it as a present?
你可以幫把它包裝成禮物嗎？

例 OK, sir. Would you wait for a second?
好的，先生。能請你稍等一下嗎？

例 Sure.
好的。

Unit 17

退換貨

8
購
物

►句型A◄

● I need to exchange it.
我需要更換。

● I'd like to return it.
我想要退貨。

● Can I have a refund?
我可以辦理退款嗎？

● This product is broken.
這商品壞了。

● I've found some defects in this product.
我發現這個商品有瑕疵。

● There is a stain on this wallet.
皮夾上有個汙點。

● This clothing is flawed.
這件衣服有瑕疵。

● It's the wrong size.
它的尺寸不對。

會話實例

例 I'd like to return it. This product is broken.

我想要退貨，這商品壞了。

例 Do you have the receipt?

你有帶收據嗎？

▶**句型 B**◀

● Do you have the receipt?

你有帶收據嗎？

● May I see your receipt?

我可以看你的收據嗎？

● What's wrong with it?

它有什麼問題。

● Would you like to have a refund?

你要辦理退款嗎？

會話實例

例 Hi. I need to exchange it.

嗨，我需要更換。

例 What's wrong with it?

它有什麼問題？

例 I bought this watch here a few days ago, but now it's not working.

我幾天前在這裡買了這支手錶，但現在它壞了。

例 May I see your receipt?

我可以看你的收據嗎？

例 Sure.

當然。

例 I'll check it to see what the problem is.

我會檢查一下看是什麼問題。

track 08-18

你一定要聽懂的 10 句話

1. What are you looking for?
   你在找什麼嗎？
2. What is your size?
   你穿什麼尺寸？
3. What color do you like?
   你要哪一個顏色？
4. Would you like to try it on?
   你要試穿看看嗎？

5. This comes in many colors.
   還有很多顏色。

6. What style would you like to see?
   你想要看哪種款式？

7. Would you like to buy it?
   你要買嗎？

8. Do you need a receipt?
   你需要收據嗎？

9. Here's the change.
   零錢在這裡。

10. What's wrong with it?
   它有什麼問題。

你一定要會說的 10 句話

1. I'm just looking around.
   我只是隨便看看。

2. I'd like to see some sport watches.
   我想看一些運動錶。

3. Would you show me how it works?
   你可以操作給我看嗎？

4. Does it have a warranty?
   這個有保固期嗎？

5. I'll take it.
   我要買！
6. Let me think about it.
   讓我考慮一下。
7. Is it possible to get a discount?
   可以打折嗎？
8. Can I have a receipt?
   可以給我收據嗎？

9. Could you wrap it up for me?
   你能幫我打包嗎？
10. I'd like to return it.
    我想要退貨。

觀光

∩ track 09-01

Unit 1 詢問旅遊資訊

▶ 句型 A ◀

- Where is the tourist information center?
  遊客服務中心在哪呢？

- Can you tell me where I can get some sightseeing information?
  你可以告訴我哪裡可以得到觀光資訊嗎？

- What time do you close?
  你們幾點關門？

- Do you have brochures?
  你們有小冊子嗎？

- I need some sightseeing information.
  我需要一些觀光資料。

- I'd like to find out more about places to visit here.
  我想要找更多關於這裡的參觀地點。

- May I take these?
  我可以拿這些嗎？

會話實例

例 Can you tell me where I can get some sightseeing information?

你可以告訴我哪裡可以得到觀光資訊嗎？

例 There's a tourist information center near the train station.

火車站附近有個遊客服務中心。

▶ 句型 B ◀

● We have many brochures here at the hotel.

我們飯店這裡有很多小冊子。

● There's a tourist information center near the train station.

火車站附近有個遊客服務中心。

● Have a look.

看看吧。

會話實例

例 Do you have Chinese brochures?

你們有中文的小冊子嗎？

例 Yes, over there.

有的，在那裡。

例 Are they free?

他們是免費的嗎？

例 Yes, they are. Have a look.

是的，看看吧。

🎧 track 09-02

詢問行程

▶ 句型 A ◀

● Are there any guided tours available here?

這裡有導覽的行程嗎？

● I'd like to find about a tour of the city.

我想找個市區觀光之旅。

● Do you have city tours?

你們有市區觀光嗎？

● How long is the tour?

行程是多久呢？

● Can we join the next tour?

我們能參加下一個行程嗎？

● How many people are in the group?

多少人參加這個團呢？

- When will they pick me up?
  他們何時會來接我？

- Are there free tours?
  有自由參觀的行程嗎？

會話實例

例 I'd like to find about a tour of the city.
我想找個市區觀光之旅。

例 We have several choices.
我們有好幾個選擇。

▶句型 B◀

- We can arrange that for you.
  我們可以幫你安排。

- The tours are free.
  導覽行程是免費的。

- The park has guided tours.
  公園有解說導覽。

- They start every half hour.
  每半個小時開始。

- A shuttle bus will take you.
  接駁車會來載你。

會話實例

例 Do you have one day tour to Redwood State Park?

你們有紅木州立公園一日遊嗎？

例 We can arrange that for you.

我們可以幫你安排。

例 What transportation is available?

有什麼交通工具可以用呢？

例 A shuttle bus will take you.

接駁車會來載你。

track 09-03

Unit 3

行程路線、時間

▶句型 A◀

● Does this tour include the art gallery?

旅遊行程有包括美術館嗎？

● Will we visit the City Hall?

我們會參觀市政府嗎？

● What is included in this tour?

旅遊行程包含哪些？

 9 觀光

- Does this tour include Niagara Falls?
  這個行程有包含尼加拉瓜大瀑布嗎？
- Does this tour go to the National Park?
  這個旅遊行程有去國家公園嗎？
- How many days does this city tour take?
  這個市區行程要多久的時間？
- How many hours does it take?
  要花幾個小時的時間？

會話實例

例 Does this tour include the art gallery?
旅遊行程有包括美術館嗎？

例 No, it just passes by it.
沒有，只有經過。

▶句型 B◀

- It'll take 2 days.
  兩天。
- What's your budget?
  你們的預算是多少？

會話實例

例 What's your budget?
你們的預算是多少？

例 Not too much. It's about $50.

不太多。大約50元。

例 OK. Here's my suggestion. You may join the city tour.

好，這是我的建議，你可以參加城市觀光行程。

例 What's the cost?

費用是多少？

例 The two-day trip price is $54.

兩天行程是54元。

 ∩ track 09-04

Unit
4

旅遊團費用明細

▶ 句型 A ◀

- What's the price of the half-day tour?

  半天的旅遊行程要多少錢？

- What's the price for that tour?

  那個旅遊行程多少錢？

- What's the price of the full-day city tour?

  市區一日遊的費用是多少？

- How much will it cost for kids?

  小孩子要多少錢？

- What's the price for an adult?
  大人要多少？

- Are there any meals included?
  有包含餐點嗎？

- Is there a pick-up service at the hotel?
  有沒有到飯店接送的服務呢？

- Does it include an English speaking guide?
  有包括會說英文的導遊嗎？

會話實例

例 What's the price of the half-day tour?
半天的旅遊行程要多少錢？

例 It's 30 Euro for one person.
一人三十歐元。

▶句型 B◀

- Here's the registration form.
  這是註冊表格。

- Please fill it in.
  請填寫。

- Please fill in the application form.
  請填寫申請表格。

會話實例

例 I'd like to join this city night tour.
我要參加市區夜間旅遊。

例 OK. Here's the registration form.
好的，這是註冊表格。

例 Is the tour all-inclusive?
行程有包括所有費用嗎？

例 Yes, the round-trip fare, and the meals are included.
是的，包括來回車資和餐費。

Unit
5

track 09-05

看秀、買票

▶**句型A**◀

● What show do you want to see tonight?
你今晚想看什麼？

會話實例

例 What show do you want to see tonight?
你今晚想看什麼？

例 I don't know. There are so many to choose from.

我不知道,有這麼多可以選。

例 Maybe we should look at some reviews.

我們或許該看些評論

▶ 句型 B ◀

● There are great Broadway shows.

有很棒的百老匯秀。

● What's the admission fee?

門票是多少?

● What opera is performing tonight?

今晚上演哪一部歌劇?

● We need to call and check on ticket availability and prices.

我們也該打電話查一下有沒有票及價錢。

● What time does this show start?

這場秀什麼時候開始?

● What time does this show end?

這場秀什麼時候結束?

會話實例

例 We need to call and check on ticket availability and prices.

我也該打電話查一下有沒有票及價錢。

例 Yes. Popular shows sell out quickly.
對，受歡迎的秀很快就賣完了。

track 09-06

Unit 6

博物館

▶句型 A◀

- Is the ticket window here?
  這裡是售票窗口嗎？

- Is there any audio guide information
  available for this place?
  這地方有錄音導覽可以用嗎？

- I need an audio guide.
  我需要錄音導覽機。

- Do you have a written guide for here?
  你們有書面介紹嗎？

- How do you turn it on?
  怎樣開機呢？

- This player does not work.
  這個導覽機壞了。

- Is there a floor map?
  有樓面圖嗎？

會話實例

例 Is there any audio guide information available for this place?
這地方有錄音導覽可以用嗎?

例 You can rent an audio guide for a fee.
你可以付費租借錄音導覽機。

▶ **句型 B** ◀

● Welcome to the Lanwell Museum.
歡迎光臨廉威爾博物館。

● There is no charge to enter our museum.
進入我們的博物館不用收費。

● You can rent an audio guide for a fee.
你可以付費租借錄音導覽機。

● Just look at the number of the display then press the number.
只要看展示品上的編號,然後按下號碼。

會話實例

例 How do you use this player.
這個導覽機要怎麼使用?

例 It's like a remote control. Just look at the number of the display then press the number.

就像遙控器一樣，只要看展示品上的編號，然後按下號碼。

 ∩track 09-07

動物園、遊樂園

▶ 句型 **A** ◀

● How much is the entry fee?
入園費是多少呢？

● Can we take pictures in the zoo?
我們可以在動物園裡拍照嗎？

● What time do you close the park?
你們幾點關閉園區呢？

● Does the pass allow us to ride and enter everything in the park?
通行證可以乘坐每樣東西及進入園區所有地方嗎？

● Is this the line for that ride?
這是坐那個的隊伍嗎？

● Where does the line start?
隊伍是從哪裡開始排的？

- Can children ride this one?
  小孩可以坐這個嗎？

會話實例

- Is the zoo open very late?
  動物園開到很晚嗎？

- It's open until eight p.m. today.
  今天開到晚上八點。

▶句型B◀

- It's open until six p.m. today.
  今天開到晚上六點。

- Please don't use flash.
  請不要用閃光燈。

- The park closes at 11:00 p.m.
  園區開到十一點。

會話實例

例 Can we take pictures in the zoo?
  我們可以在動物園裡拍照嗎？

例 Yes, but please don't use flash.
  可以，但請不要用閃光燈。

Unit 8 海上活動

▶ 句型 A ◀

- Is it safe to swim here?
  在這裡游泳安全嗎？

- Is it OK to swim here?
  這裡可以游泳嗎？

- Is there a lifeguard here?
  這裡有救生員嗎？

- I need a life vest.
  我需要救生衣。

- We need some float rings and kick boards.
  我需要一些游泳圈跟浮板。

- Let' get some snorkeling equipment.
  我們來找一些浮潛用具吧。

- We want to rent some skis.
  我們想要租一些水上摩托車。

會話實例

例 Is it safe to swim here?
在這裡游泳安全嗎？

例 You must be careful of the undertow.
你要小心暗流。

▶ 句型 B ◀

● There are many lifeguards here.
這裡有很多救生員。

● Stay in the marked arcas.
待在標示的區域內。

會話實例

例 Is there a lifeguard here?
這裡有救生員嗎？

例 There are many lifeguards here.
這裡有很多救生員。

 ∩ track 09-09

Unit
9
參加晚宴

▶ 句型 A ◀

● Welcome.
歡迎。

● It's so nice to see you.
見到你真好。

3
2
4

- Come in and let me fix you a drink.

  請進，我幫你弄杯飲料。

- We are happy you could come.

  我們很高興你能來。

- You are welcome here anytime.

  歡迎你隨時來。

會話實例

例 Welcome. It's so nice to see you.

歡迎，見到你真好。

例 Thank you. It's so nice to see you, too.

謝謝，見到你也很棒。

▶句型 B◀

- Here is something I brought for tonight's dinner.

  這是我為今天晚餐買的東西。

- I brought a bottle of wine.

  我買了一瓶酒。

- Thanks for inviting me.

  謝謝你邀我來。

- I want to thank you for inviting me to dinner.

  我要感謝你們邀我來晚餐。

● The dinner was great.
晚餐很棒。

● It's been fun.
今晚很好玩。

● I hope I can return the favor sometime.
希望改天能回請你們。

● I hope we can do it again soon.
希望很快可以再聚會。

會話實例

例 I want to thank you for inviting me to dinner.
我要感謝你們邀我來晚餐。

例 We are happy you could come.
我們很高興你能來。

 ∩ track 09-10

Unit 10
拍照

▶句型A◀

● Excuse me.
不好意思。

- Would you take a picture of us?
  能請你幫我們拍張照嗎？

- Press this button.
  按這個鈕。

- Just aim and shoot.
  只要瞄準及拍攝。

- Let's use the flash.
  我們用閃光燈吧。

- It didn't flash.
  閃光燈沒亮。

- Please take one more.
  請多照一張。

- May I take a photo of all of you?
  我可以拍一張你們的全體照嗎？

9
觀
光

會話實例

例 Would you take a picture of us?
　能請你幫我們拍張照嗎？

例 Sure. How do you use this camera?
　當然，你這相機怎麼用呢？

▶句型 B◀

- How do you use this camera?
  你這相機怎麼用呢？

- Are you ready?
  準備好了嗎？

- Let me help you take a picture.
  我來幫你們拍張照。

會話實例

例 How do you use this camera?
你這相機怎麼用呢？

例 It's simple. Just aim and press this button.
很簡單，只要瞄準及按這個鈕。

🎧 track 09-11

你一定要聽懂的10句話

1. There's a tourist information center near the train station.
   火車站附近有個遊客服務中心。

2. We can arrange that for you.
   我們可以幫你安排。

3. The park has guided tours.
   公園有解說導覽。

4. What's your budget?
   你們的預算是多少？
5. Please fill in the application form.
   請填寫申請表格。
6. You can rent an audio guide for a fee.
   你可以付費租借錄音導覽機。
7. There are many lifeguards here.
   這裡有很多救生員。
8. Stay in the marked areas.
   待在標示的區域內。
9. We are happy you could come.
   我們很高興你能來。
10. You are welcome here anytime.
    歡迎你隨時來。
11. How do you use this camera?
    你這相機怎麼用呢？

9 觀光

你一定要會說的 10 句話

1. Where is the tourist information center?
   遊客服務中心在哪呢？
2. Are there any guided tours available here?
   這裡有導覽的行程嗎？

3. What sights do you recommend?

   你推薦哪一些觀光點？

4. What is included in this tour?

   旅遊行程包含哪些？

5. I need an audio guide.

   我需要錄音導覽機。

6. What time do you close the park?

   你們幾點關閉園區呢？

7. Is it safe to swim here?

   在這裡游泳安全嗎？

8. Where is a good place to go to at night?

   晚上有哪個地方好去呢？

9. Thanks for inviting me.

   謝謝你邀我來

10. Would you take a picture of us?

    能請你幫我們拍張照嗎？

Chapter

10

急救、生病、
意外狀況

🎧track 10-01

Unit 1
迷路

▶句型 **A** ◀

- Excuse me.
  不好意思。

- I'm lost.
  我迷路了。

- I don't know where I am.
  我不知道我在哪裡。

- Where am I on this map?
  我在地圖上的什麼地方？

- Where am I?
  我在哪？

- I'm looking for the Peterson Building.
  我在找彼德森大樓。

- Would you show me how to get there?
  你可以跟我講怎麼去嗎？

- Is this the way to the railway station?
  這是去火車站的方向嗎？

⑩ 急救、生病、意外狀況

會話實例

例 Excuse me. I'm lost.
不好意思。我迷路了。

例 Where do you want to go?
你要去哪裡？

▶句型 B◀

● May I help you?
你需要幫忙嗎？

● Where do you want to go?
你要去哪裡？

● You're going the wrong way.
你走錯方向了。

● You need to go the other way about six blocks.
你要往另一頭走大約六個街區。

● Turn right and you will see it.
右轉你就會看到。

● It's at the end of this street.
在這條街的盡頭。

● Turn right and go straight ahead.
右轉然後直走。

● You're right here, near the station.
你在這裡，火車站旁。

會話實例

例 Where am I on this map?
我在地圖上的什麼地方？

例 You're right here, near the station.
你在這裡，火車站旁。

track 10-02

Unit 2

尋求協助

▶句型A◀

● Please do me a favor.
請幫我一個忙。

● Give me a hand, please?
請幫我一個忙。

● Would you please help me?
你可以幫我嗎？

● I need your help.
我需要你的幫忙。

- If it's not too much trouble, I'd like some help.

  如果不麻煩，我需要你的幫忙。

- Could you get that bag for me?

  你可以幫我拿那個包包嗎？

- Can you keep an cyc on my bag, please?

  你能幫我顧一下包包嗎？

會話實例

例 Please do me a favor.

請幫我一個忙。

例 What is it?

什麼忙？

例 Can you keep an eye on my bag, please?

你能幫我顧一下包包嗎？

▶句型 B◀

- Do you need any help?

  你需要幫忙嗎？

- Is there anything I can do?

  有沒有我可以做的？

- Let me help you with it.

  讓我來幫你。

- I'll get this bag for you.
  我幫你拿袋子。

- Would you like me to get you a cab?
  你需要我幫你叫計程車嗎？

- It's no trouble at all.
  一點都不麻煩。

會話實例

例 Let me help you with it.
讓我來幫你。

例 Thank you so much.
非常感謝你。

♪track 10-03

Unit 3

呼救

▶句型 A◀

- Help!
  救命阿！

- Call an ambulance!
  叫救護車！

- Please call 911.
  請報警。

- Please call the police for me.
  請幫我報警。

- Somebody, help me.
  來人啊！救救我！

- Anybody here?
  有人在嗎？

- Fire.
  發生火災了！

- There is a boy in the river.
  有個男孩掉到河裡了！

會話實例

例 Help!
　救命阿！

例 What happened?
　發生什麼事？

▶句型B◀

- What happened?
  發生什麼事？

- I'll get someone to help you.
  我會找人來幫你。

會話實例

- Oh my god!
  我的天哪！

- What happened?
  發生什麼事？

- Call an ambulance!
  叫救護車！

 ∩ track 10-04

Unit
4
報警

► 句型 A ◄

- I want to report a crime.
  我要報案。

- Someone stole my wallet.
  有人偷了我的皮夾。

- I was assaulted.
  我被攻擊了。

- I want to report an emergency.
  我要報告緊急事件。

- Will an officer come soon?
  警員很快會過來嗎？

⑩ 急救、生病、意外狀況

會話實例

例 I want to report a crime.

我要報案。

例 What happened?

發生什麼事？

例 Someone stole my wallet.

有人偷了我的皮夾。

▶句型 B◀

- What happened?

  發生什麼事？

- Can you describe the person?

  你可以描述一下那個人嗎？

- When and where did this happen?

  什麼時候和在哪發生的？

- Did you notice anything else?

  你還有注意到別的嗎？

- Just sit here and relax.

  請坐在這裡放輕鬆。

- If you think of anything else, let me know.

  如果你還想到什麼就告訴我。

會話實例

例 What happened?

發生什麼事？

例 Someone robbed my backpack.

有人搶了我的包包！

例 Can you describe the person?

你可以描述一下那個人嗎？

例 He was wearing a black coat and jeans.

他穿一件黑色外套和牛仔褲。

 ∩ track 10-05

Unit 5
失物招領

▶ 句型 A ◀

● I lost my wallet.

我的皮夾不見了。

● I want to give this to the Lost and Found.

我要把這個交給失物招領處。

● I think someone lost it.

我想有人弄丟了這個。

- Did someone find my wallet?
  有人找到我的錢包嗎？

會話實例

例 I lost my wallet.
我的皮夾不見了。

例 When did you lose it?
你什麼時候掉的？

例 Yesterday afternoon.
昨天下午。

▶句型 B◀

- Did you go to the Lost and Found?
  你有去失物招領處嗎？

- When did you lose it?
  你什麼時候掉的？

- Two wallets were turned in yesterday.
  昨天有兩個錢包被交過來。

- You'll have to describe it to me.
  你要對我形容一下你的皮夾。

會話實例

例 Did someone find my wallet?
有人找到我的錢包嗎？

例 You'll have to describe it to me.

你要對我形容一下你的皮夾。

例 It's a black wallet.

是個黑色的皮夾。

生病

▶句型 A◀

● I'd like to see a doctor.

我要看醫生。

● I feel ill.

我生病了。

● I have a stomachache.

我胃痛。

● I have a headache.

我頭痛。

● I have toothache.

我牙齒痛。

● I feel very dizzy.

我頭很暈。

- I feel faint.
  我快暈倒了。

- I need something to kill the pain.
  我需要點什麼東西來止痛。

會話實例

例 Tell me what is wrong.
告訴我怎麼了。

例 I have a stomachache.
我胃痛。

▶句型 B◀

- Do you have an appointment?
  你有預約嗎？

- Tell me what is wrong.
  告訴我怎麼了。

- I'm going to take your temperature.
  我要幫你量體溫。

- I think you have the flu.
  你感冒了。

- You have a slight fever.
  你有點發燒。

- You need a shot.
  你要打針。

- Are you allergic to penicillin?
  你會對盤尼西林過敏嗎？

- You need to stay at the hospital over-night.
  你今晚需要住院。

會話實例

例 Tell me what is wrong.
告訴我怎麼了。

例 I threw up twice in the morning.
我早上吐了兩次。

🎧 track 10-07

你一定要聽懂的 10 句話

1. Where do you want to go?
   你要去哪裡？

2. You're going the wrong way.
   你走錯方向了。

3. Do you need any help?
   你需要幫忙嗎？

4. Let me help you with it.
   讓我來幫你。

5. What happened?
   發生什麼事？

6. Can you describe the person?
   你可以描述一下那個人嗎？

7. When and where did this happen?
   什麼時候和在哪發生的？

8. Did you go to the Lost and Found?
   你有去失物招領處嗎？

9. Tell me what is wrong.
   告訴我怎麼了。

10. Three times a day after meals.
    三餐飯後食用。

你一定要會說的10句話

1. I'm lost.
   我迷路了。

2. Where am I on this map?
   我在地圖上的什麼地方？

3. Please do me a favor.
   請幫我一個忙。

4. Help!
   救命啊！

5. Call an ambulance!
   叫救護車！
6. Please call 911.
   請報警。
7. I want to report a crime.
   我要報案。
8. I lost my wallet.
   我的皮夾不見了。
9. I want to give this to the Lost and Found.
   我要把這個交給失物招領處。
10. I'd like to see a doctor.
    我要看醫生。

⑩ 急救、生病、意外狀況

永續圖書
線上購物網

www.foreverbooks.com.tw

◆ 加入會員即享活動及會員折扣。

◆ 每月均有優惠活動，期期不同。

◆ 新加入會員三天內訂購書籍不限本數金額，
   即贈送精選書籍一本。（依網站標示為主）

專業圖書發行、書局經銷、圖書出版

永續圖書總代理：
五觀藝術出版社、培育文化、棋茵出版社、犬拓文化、讀
品文化、雅典文化、知音人文化、手藝家出版社、瑧申文
化、智學堂文化、語言鳥文化

活動期內，永續圖書將保留變更或終止該活動之權利及最終決定權。

就是這一本，超實用的旅遊英語

雅致風靡 典藏文化

親愛的顧客您好，感謝您購買這本書。即日起，填寫讀者回函卡寄回至本公司，我們每月將抽出一百名回函讀者，寄出精美禮物並享有生日當月購書優惠！想知道更多更即時的消息，歡迎加入"永續圖書粉絲團"您也可以選擇傳真、掃描或用本公司準備的免郵回函寄回，謝謝。

傳真電話：（02）8647-3660　　　　電子信箱：yungjiuh@ms45.hinet.net

姓名：		性別：　□男　□女
出生日期：　年　　月　　日		電話：
學歷：		職業：
E-mail：		
地址：□□□		
從何處購買此書：		購買金額：　　　元

購買本書動機：□封面 □書名 □排版 □內容 □作者 □偶然衝動

你對本書的意見：
內容：□滿意□尚可□待改進　　編輯：□滿意□尚可□待改進
封面：□滿意□尚可□待改進　　定價：□滿意□尚可□待改進

其他建議：

總經銷：永續圖書有限公司

永續圖書線上購物網
www.foreverbooks.com.tw

您可以使用以下方式將回函寄回。

您的回覆，是我們進步的最大動力，謝謝。

① 使用本公司準備的免郵回函寄回。

② 傳真電話：（02）8647-3660

③ 掃描圖檔寄到電子信箱：

　　yungjiuh@ms45.hinet.net

沿此線對折後寄回，謝謝。

雅致風靡　典藏文化